TAKING SIDES

I felt funny. I wondered if Greta knew I liked Daddy best, better than Mom. I do. I know it's awful, but I always have. They always say you're supposed to love both your parents equally, but maybe you can't always. Just like I don't think parents always love both their children equally. I know Mom, for instance, loves Hugo better than me. She always says he's like an animal, a cub, sort of roly-poly and wild, and I'm too quiet and serious. But, still, I feel badly that I love Daddy the most.

"Did you mind?" I said.

"Mind what?"

"Loving him the most, your father?"

Greta was chewing on a long piece of grass. Finally she said, "You just can't program who you're going to love, Nell—it happens, that's all. You can love a flower, a stone, a person, a dog. . . . There's nothing you can do about it."

I don't know what I think about that, if I agree or not. I have to think about it.

Taking Sides

NORMA KLEIN

AVON
PUBLISHERS OF BARD, CAMELOT AND DISCUS BOOKS

AVON BOOKS
A division of
The Hearst Corporation
959 Eighth Avenue
New York, New York 10019

Copyright © 1974 by Norma Klein
Published by arrangement with Pantheon Books
Library of Congress Catalog Card Number: 74-972
ISBN: 0-380-00528-X

First Avon Printing, February, 1976
Fourth Printing

AVON TRADEMARK REG. U.S. PAT. OFF. AND
FOREIGN COUNTRIES, REGISTERED TRADEMARK—
MARCA REGISTRADA, HECHO EN CHICAGO, U.S.A.

Printed in the U.S.A.

To Bob and Deborah

Taking Sides

Chapter One

"I decided to come after all," I said.

Mom and her friend Greta looked up. They had been sitting with their backs to me watching Hugo, who was playing at the side of the lake. I guess they were afraid he might just wander off the way he sometimes does. Hugo's five and tells everyone he can swim, but he really can't.

"I'm glad you changed your mind, hon," Mom said, "only we've eaten everything up. We made pigs of ourselves."

"I'll just pick at a bone or something," I said. I knew Mom had made a fried chicken, even though Greta is a vegetarian and won't eat any meat, except fish.

"Whew, it's hot," Greta said. She looked at me and smiled. "I saw you up on the hill."

Greta is an old friend of Mom's, from college. I guess she's as old as Mom, thirty-four or thirty-seven or something like that. She's always watching things. She's just that kind of person. Sometimes it makes me nervous.

"I was just thinking," I said quickly. In fact, I like sitting and watching people, knowing they can't see me. From a distance they had hardly looked like people, just clumps of color: Mom in her striped purple and red tent dress, Greta in her denim shirt and jeans and her big floppy straw hat. Greta's skin is very light—she says she can't take the sun and always wears her hat, especially when she's gardening.

"Hugo, stay up on the shore," Mom called. "Oh help! I'd better get him." She ambled off while I began munching on a leftover chicken bone.

"What were you thinking about?" Greta asked, half turning to look at me.

I shrugged. "Oh, just this year . . . how it will be."

"Are you scared?" Greta said.

"Noo."

Greta was looking down at Mom and Hugo. "I think new things are always scary," she said.

That's something I like about Greta. She'll admit right away to feeling scared the way most grown-ups won't. "When I was your age," she said, "I was younger actually—what are you—eleven?"

"Twelve," I said.

"When I was ten, my mother died and I lived just with my father. It was all right . . . in fact, it was wonderful, but I wasn't sure it would be then."

"What did your mother die of?" I asked.

"T.B. Oh, she was sick all the time when I was a child—I used to come in and sit on her bed and we'd do quiet playing, you know, reading and stuff, but—then she just died."

"That must have been awful." I can't even imagine Mom dying. Not living with her is one thing —but not having her there at all would be really terrible.

"It was . . . in a way," Greta said, "but I really loved my father best, I always did. So that made it not so bad." She looked carefully at me. Greta is very tall and thin. She has light hair which she wears in braids, and millions of freckles, so many

10

it's almost like a tan. Her eyes are blue, just like the eyes of her cat, Tangiers, and she has a croggy sort of voice which Mom says is from smoking too much. Mom says Greta should stop smoking, but she won't.

I felt funny. I wondered if Greta knew I liked Daddy best, better than Mom. I do. I know it's awful, but I always have. They always say you're supposed to love both your parents equally, but maybe you can't always. Just like I don't think parents always love both their children equally. I know Mom, for instance, loves Hugo better than me. She always says he's like an animal, a cub, sort of roly-poly and wild, and I'm too quiet and serious. But, still, I feel badly that I love Daddy the most.

"Did you mind?" I said.

"Mind what?"

"Loving him the most, your father?"

Greta was chewing on a long piece of grass. Finally she said, "You just can't program who you're going to love, Nell—it happens, that's all. You can love a flower, a stone, a person, a dog. . . . There's nothing you can do about it."

I don't know what I think about that, if I agree or not. I have to think about it. Heather, my best friend who lives in New York, would probably agree with Greta. She believes in horoscopes and she's always saying I'm too practical. Maybe I am. Daddy is practical too. I think that's why we've always gotten along.

Mom and Hugo were playing down by the water. I don't even know if Hugo knows that in three days, after Labor Day, we'll be going back to New York, to live with Daddy in a new apartment. These past two months, since Mom and Daddy got divorced, we've stayed out here in New Jersey at Greta's house. Mom hates the city and Greta said she could live here with her if she liked. Of course, Mom has to commute into the city for her

11

job, but for the last month she's had vacation and we've all been together.

Hugo is sort of oblivious to the change in our lives. It must be funny being under six. I can hardly remember back that far. I can remember first grade and everything since then pretty well, but I can hardly remember when I was five. Hugo wasn't even born then. I was living with Mom in Boston. It's strange—Mom and Daddy got divorced when I was five, then they got married again when I was seven, and now they're divorced all over again. I remember the time they got remarried. It was in the backyard of Grandma Rose's house. Mom wore a garland of flowers around her head and Daddy had one around his neck. They said they wanted a real wedding since the first time they just went to City Hall in regular clothes, not even a wedding dress for Mom or anything. The first time they got married they were just in college. Mom was a freshman and Daddy was a senior.

"I'm going to swim," Greta said, leaping up. She always moves quickly, jumping to her feet in one motion. "Want to come, Nell?"

"Maybe in a second."

Greta smiled. "It'll be okay," she said.

"Oh sure," I said quickly. I don't like Mom and Daddy to know I worry about things, but really I do. I want to live with Daddy, I think it will be good, it just seems odd. Everyone else I know who has parents that are divorced lives with their mother. But Mom works every day—she's a computer programmer—and Hugo still isn't in school except in the morning, and Daddy works at home—he's a free-lance science-book writer—so I guess it seemed easier for Daddy to do it. I don't know. They just said that was how it would be, we'd come out here to New Jersey on weekends, Hugo and me, and we'd be together Christmas and things like that.

I walked down to the lake. Greta said, "I'm going to take everything off. It's too hot." In about one second she was naked and splashing into the lake.

"Me too," Hugo yelled. "I want everything off!"

"Okay, baby. Take it easy." Mom yanked off Hugo's clothes and he went crashing into the water, yelping. Then Mom, sort of slowly, as though she were thinking of something else, pulled off her tent dress and waded in. Mom is sort of chubby. She reminds me of those old-fashioned china dolls in Greta's parents' house with big- black eyes and round red cheeks and black hair flat all around with bangs. She has big breasts, Greta has hardly any. "Are you going to come in, hon?" Mom said, turning to look at me.

"Maybe." I feel funny undressing in front of people, even people like Mom and Greta whom I know. My figure isn't bad. I'm not especially fat or thin, I just don't have much of anything like breasts and that sort of thing. I waited until they were all in swimming and then quickly pulled everything off and jumped in so fast no one could see me.

It was great. The lake connects to a stream and it's always really cold, partly because trees hang over on both sides and there isn't much sun. I lay on my back, looking up at the trees. The water was so cold and kept running over me. It felt like it was running through me, like I was just hollow. I could feel my hair streaming out behind me. I love lying on my back in the water. I've never been good at putting my face in. I just lay there, letting my body drift downstream.

All of a sudden Hugo came splashing over and yanked my hair. I started to go under and water went up my nose which is something I really hate. "Go away, you pest!" I yelled. "Leave me alone."

"I want a ride," he yelled.

"Well, you're not getting one. Go to Mommy— she'll give you one."

But Mom and Greta were already on the shore, drying off.

"Hugo, don't be a pest," Mom yelled. "Come on out, you're turning blue."

For someone who can't swim, Hugo can manage to raise a lot of mess in water. He just wouldn't let go of me till I let him hang on my back and lugged him to shore. Greta threw me a towel. Mom threw one to Hugo. "Here, Brute," she said.

Brute is Mom's pet name for Hugo. It suits him. She began tickling him and drying him at the same time, singing, "Bruto, bruto, bruto, he is a little brute! Bruto, bruto, bruto, he is a little brute!"

Hugo wouldn't even put on his clothes. He just ran yelping back to the house with not a stitch on. Luckily the house is far from the road so no one was likely to see.

Chapter Two

Greta's parents are in Florida. Her father remarried after her mother died and now they've settled in Florida and given her the house. I like it. It's a very old house, built hundreds of years ago. There's a fireplace in almost every room. The furniture is old but comfortable, and there are all kinds of interesting things Greta's stepmother collected like a set of glass mice playing musical instruments and some old puppets and a stuffed dog that Greta said her stepmother kept intending to give away but never did. Right outside the house is a tree with bells in it. Greta bought the bells in India when she was there. When the wind blows, you can hear the bells. The first week we were here, Hugo found some milkweed pods and went outside with them. When I asked him what he was doing, he said, "I want to show them to the bells."

My room has two beds, a double one and a regular. Mom says if I want, Heather can come and stay sometimes. I bet Heather would like it. She loves the outdoors and nature. I think I'm more a city person. I wouldn't like to live here all year round, even though it's nice for the summer.

"Help Greta in the garden, Nell, will you?" Mom said, "I want to get Hugo packed off."

Greta's garden is huge. I guess it has to be because if you're a vegetarian, all you can eat is vegetables. The funny thing is that Greta will eat fish. She loves to fish. And to me that's just as cruel as killing a cow. Greta says it's not just a matter of principles, she likes vegetables a lot. I'm glad Mom eats meat, though, and lets me.

"Would you like me to help?" I asked Greta.

She looked up, a raw carrot sticking out of her mouth like a cigarette. "Oh, go set the table if you feel like being useful."

Greta likes to be by herself—I knew she wouldn't want me out there. So I set the table. We eat in the kitchen at this round wooden table. I wonder if I would like to live in the same place my parents did, all my life. Greta doesn't seem to mind. She says she couldn't afford a place like this on her own and she hates the city, like Mom. I think it would be funny to sleep in the same bed you had when you were little. I wouldn't like it.

After I set the table, I sat down and wrote to Heather. We don't write much, but since I'll see her in three days, I thought I would. I don't even know what our new phone number will be. I've never seen our apartment. Daddy picked it over the summer and then went away.

The phone rang. I waited a little but since nobody answered it, I picked it up. It was Daddy.

I got so excited I sat down. "Are you in New York?"

"Yes, I've been back since Sunday."

Back since Sunday! A whole week almost. I wonder why he didn't call right away.

"How are things going, love?"

"Oh, okay. Did you have a nice trip, Daddy?"

"Pretty good . . . I'm glad to be back." Daddy always says he hates vacations, can't relax. Mom says that's because he's too compulsive about his work.

"When are you coming out?"

"Out where?"

"Aren't you coming out to get us?"

"Oh—no, I thought Phyllis would bring you in Sunday night."

"Oh . . . I just didn't know. Does Mom know?"

"Let me speak to her."

I went upstairs to get Mom. She was reading to Hugo. There are about three books Hugo likes— *Babar, Curious George* and *The Little Engine that Could*. You can go crazy reading those books over and over to him. "Nell, would you finish up with Hugo?" Mom said, going for the phone.

I sat down on Hugo's bed. Luckily, they were almost at the end of the book. Hugo smelled nice. Mom must have given him his bath. Hugo really is cute, I guess, if it weren't for his personality. He has this big round head with lots of blond curls and big blue eyes. He's the kind of child grownups are always patting on the head. Actually, he can be very quiet at times, when he's not being really wild. He's usually one or the other, not in between like most people. I read him the rest of the story. He said, "I want Mommy to come back."

"She's on the phone with Daddy."

Hugo looked at me. "What for?"

"Because we're going home Sunday. They have to decide how."

"Going home?"

"Hugo, come on, you know. We're going back to New York . . . to live with Daddy in our new place. There's school and all that, your same old school."

"Is Mommy going too?"

"No, she's going to stay here with Greta."

Hugo was staring at me like I'd just told him we were going to fly to the moon on Sunday. I couldn't believe it. We've talked about all this millions of times. "I want to stay with Mommy and Greta," he said.

17

"Well, you can't . . . Mommy has to work."

"I'm going to live with Mommy," Hugo said. "You live with Daddy."

Frankly, I'd love that. I wish we could do it. But we can't. "Okay—well—talk about it with Mommy, okay?"

Hugo was looking out the window. "The bells are going," he said.

"Yes, isn't that nice?"

"This is a nice place," he said.

"We'll visit them," I said, trying again. "We'll come at Christmas. We can go out and chop down our own Christmas tree."

"We can?"

Hugo was looking so happy, but I didn't know if he really got the point. But Mom came back. "It's all set," she said.

I went downstairs again.

Greta was in the kitchen washing vegetables. Sometimes she makes them taste very hot by adding curry and then we have yogurt with it to cool it off, but this time she said it would be just plain. "That was Daddy," I said, "on the phone before."

She just nodded.

After supper Mom played the piano and Greta played her flute. Greta still takes flute lessons, even though she's a grownup. She says she likes the oboe best, but an oboe costs six hundred dollars so she just has a flute. It's a silver-plated flute, not a real silver one, but it sounds very nice. Mom sight reads, so she has to go slow and sometimes she makes mistakes.

"Count, idiot!" Greta yelled suddenly.

"I *am*," said Mom.

"You're not. Now, Phyll, you have to, listen to me . . . it's important."

"Don't be so strict," I said. I was lying on the couch with an afghan over me, half listening.

"There . . . you heard the girl," Mom said.

"If we're going to play, let's do it right," Greta

18

said. But she sat for a minute, holding her flute. "If you two think I'm strict, you should meet my flute teacher. She's a maniac. She used to make me cry almost, she was so strict."

It's hard to imagine Greta crying. "What did you do?" I said.

"Well, finally I told her, I said she just made me feel awful and it wasn't nice and the funny part was she didn't even realize she'd been that way. Ever since then we've been good friends."

"One should always say things," Mom said, sighing.

Heather always says that too. I agree, but it's hard to say things. I guess I'm like Daddy, sort of repressed. I hate to tell people things right out. Like, if I was Greta, I could never have said that to the flute teacher. I would probably just have stopped taking lessons from her.

"Is Daddy coming out for us," I asked Mom, "on Sunday?"

"No, I'll take you both in," Mom said.

I was disappointed. I'd been looking forward to showing Daddy the house and the lake and the bells. "I wish he could see the house," I said.

"Oh, he'll see it," Mom said. "Don't worry."

"Let's start again," Greta said, "from the beginning of the second bar, okay?"

They began to play again. The flute is very cool. It reminds me of floating downstream in the lake.

Chapter Three

Greta's house has a real mailbox. To get to it you have to walk down this path a little bit and there it is, off under some trees. It has her family's name on it—Mentz. I usually go get the mail just because I like the walk. Mom and Greta sleep late on weekends—till ten or eleven, but I always get up early. Sometimes I just lie in bed, looking out the window. But usually Hugo, who gets up at the crack of dawn, comes crashing in and leaps on my bed, licking my face and shoving various books at me to read to him. Hugo can read, if pressed—he knows all the letters, but he just won't if he can get someone to read to him. And I drew him this diagram of a clock, so he'd know what seven looked like on the clock in his room. He's pretty good about not coming in before that.

I remember when I was five we lived in this apartment in New York that looked right out on another apartment with a fire escape. It was a little too far away to be able to talk from one building to another, but there was this other little girl that used to come to the window and we would show each other our toys. I never met her on the street or even found out her name.

"Hugo, want to come for the mail with me?"

Hugo gets himself dressed which is pretty good even if it is the same shorts and shirt that he's been wearing all summer, which Mom got him in about six versions. He's not too great on buttons, but who cares, really.

Hugo trailed behind on the way for the mail. He loves to gather up whatever we see on our path, sticks or special stones or old leaves. Usually, most of it gets thrown away, but Mom lets him keep some of it.

There were six letters. I let Hugo carry them back. It was going to be hot again, but now, at ten, it was still lovely and not too dusty and sticky.

"Can we wake Mommy up now?" Hugo said.

"Sure, it's late enough, I guess. Don't drop any of the letters, okay?"

Hugo raced ahead and by the time I got back to the house he was in Mom and Greta's room and had leapt on top of Mom, shoving the letters in her face. "Here, Mommy, here, Mommy," he said.

"Hugo, I see. . . . Down, boy! Aah!" Mom yawned and sank back under the covers. It takes her a long time to wake up in the morning, unlike Daddy who is always wide awake the second he gets out of bed.

Greta's bed is by the window. She was lying back with her cat, Tangiers, slung around her neck like a scarf. She was smoking. "Hi, kids," she said. In the morning her voice is even more croggy than ever.

Mom squinted at the mail. "Three Rebecca Ingersolls," she said. "Yowee zow!"

Rebecca Ingersoll isn't a real person. What happened or how she came to exist is this. Mom and Greta just for fun once wrote this Gothic novel. They did it just for fun, but the odd part was it was a big success and made quite a lot of money.

So they wrote another and now they're writing a third. Only no one is supposed to know who Rebecca Ingersoll is because she's really two people. There's never a photo of her on the book jacket. What I thought they should do is take a photo of Mom's head and Greta's body and put them all together. No one would know. But the man who put out the book didn't think that was such a good idea. The funny part is Rebecca Ingersoll gets so much mail, more than most real people ever get. There's hardly been a day all summer when she didn't get two or even three letters! I really like getting letters and I hardly ever do. It doesn't seem fair that someone who doesn't even exist should get so much mail. Usually Mom just tosses all the letters in a big basket and sometimes answers them. Greta hates opening letters.

"Can I open them, Mom?" I asked.

"Be my guest."

I sat on the edge of Greta's bed and read the first one. It was from a lady who lived in Maine and was sure that Rebecca Ingersoll must have once passed through her hometown because the description was so much like it. Especially the scene in the cemetery. She said their cemetery was just like that. There was even a gravestone like the one Teresina L'Heureux sat on when she had to figure out how to reclaim her dead aunt's legacy. I should say that all of these novels are fairly scary, though not really gruesome. Usually it's this girl or lady who goes somewhere she's never been and there are various not very nice people who almost do her in. But then there's usually one good person who helps her get free. Sometimes a person is killed, but so far it's never the main person. I'm glad. I hope they never murder off the main person.

"What's it say?" said Greta.

"Well, this lady—her name is Mrs. Maureen H. Jeffries of Lewiston, Maine—says you must have been in her hometown, especially to the cemetery."

"What cemetery?" Greta said, yawning.

"Oh Greta, come *on*, you remember," I said, "you had that scene in the cemetery where Teresina L'Heureux tries to figure out how to reclaim her dead aunt's legacy." Actually, I haven't *exactly* read the whole book, just parts.

"Can't remember a thing about it," Greta said.

That's really weird. Imagine not being able to remember your own book!

Suddenly Greta began to cough. "Nell, could you get me a glass of water?" she said.

"Greta, if you don't stop smoking!" Mom said.

"Cut it out, Phyll."

"You're killing yourself!"

"So's everyone."

"Apart from being untrue, that's a rotten excuse."

"Live your own life, will you?"

"I hate to see you suffer."

"That's suffering? Look, everyone in my family has lived a disgustingly long time. Most of them should've been shot somewhere along the line. I'm more afraid of living too long than of not living long enough."

I gave Greta her water. She gulped it down. "Thanks."

"Is that why you have such a croggy voice?" I said. "From smoking?"

"No!" said Greta. "No, really, I had this voice when I was seven and I wasn't smoking then. It's just my natural voice."

"Excuses, excuses," said Mom. She sat up and shook her head. Then she pitched all the letters into the corner of the room. "A pox on Rebecca Ingersoll!" she yelled.

"Mom!" I said. "Stop that!"

"That's telling her, Nell," said Greta. "You know, we've got to teach your mother a lesson. She's acting too silly lately."

"A pox, pox, pox on Rebecca Ingersoll!" Mom began singing in this loud, dopey way.

23

Greta, Hugo and I all went over and pounced on her and began punching her and tickling her. "Help, help," she cried, trying to hide under the covers.

"Take it back?" Greta said.

"I take it all back," Mom said, panting. Her face was all red. "I love Rebecca Ingersoll. She's a doll."

"Mom."

"What, golden girl?"

"Could I answer some of these letters to Rebecca Ingersoll?"

"Could you? I'd love it! I'll pay you! Fifty cents a letter."

"Really?" Gosh, why didn't I ask before? I would love to answer them and to get paid as well. "Can I use your typewriter?"

"Sure. The ribbon's not too great, but . . ."

"Oh, that's okay." I ran off into the study.

Greta came after me. "Don't you want breakfast, Nell?"

"I'm not hungry," I shouted. I felt too excited to eat. I really wanted to answer those letters. Maybe from now on I could answer all of them since Mom doesn't like to do it and Greta hates it, in fact. I wrote the first lady a long letter. I told her I had been in her hometown and loved it. I said I had a cousin who had lived there and was buried in that cemetery and that was what gave me the idea for that scene. After all, that *could* be true.

The second letter was harder. It was from someone from Illinois who didn't like something in one of the books. She wanted to know why Rebecca Ingersoll had a fox hunting scene when fox hunting was a barbaric sport and she had always assumed that R.I. would hate it too. I wrote her yes, I did, but people then did do fox hunting and so you had to show what it was like. I said, "I am a vegetarian and never even eat meat so you can see I would never do anything bad to animals." That's

24

true of Greta and since she is one half of Rebecca Ingersoll, it's not a lie to say that.

I spent all morning answering letters, it was so much fun. When I came out of the study it was one in the afternoon. Greta and Mom and Hugo were coming back from a walk. "I did six of them!" I said, running to meet them.

"Nell, you're a darling," Mom said. "Take three dollars out of the china kitty."

The china kitty is in the kitchen. It's where Mom and Greta keep their extra money.

"The thing is, I'm going to make Rebecca Ingersoll a real person," I said, "part of you and part of Greta—with some things mixed in. But I'll remember what I said so I won't get mixed up."

"Terrific," Greta said. "Hey, how about writing my letters for me? Would you write my father Nell? I've owed him a letter for ages."

"A real letter, you mean?"

"Oh, come on, Greta," Mom said, "how could she write a real letter for you?"

"Ya, I guess not," Greta sighed. "Too bad. It was a great idea."

Chapter Four

That night I packed. I didn't have a lot of clothes, but I stuffed everything in anyway. Mom said we would all, except Greta, go in to New York by bus tomorrow evening. Mom has a car, but she said bus would be easier with Hugo. I wish Hugo could stay with Mom. He's going to be a mess without her. She says he can't because she's away all day. I wish Greta would look after him part of the day, but she just says she won't.

"Why won't you?" I said. She was in my room stripping the beds.

"I'm not the maternal type," she said.

"But you like Hugo, don't you?" I said.

"In small doses."

"That's funny," I said.

"What is?"

"Being the maternal type . . . I thought all women liked babies, somewhat."

"Come off it, Nell . . . you know better than that. Are all your friends' mothers so great?"

"Well, no."

"Let's face it," Greta said, "to be a mother, you have to put up with an infinite amount of shit. And I don't know if I could take that."

I thought about this awhile. "Do you think Mom is the maternal type?"

"Yes, basically I do."

I wonder which type I'll be. I never really thought about it. I mean, I just imagined I would have children when I grew up. I don't think I would like to have just a cat like Greta. But I don't know if I would like to put up with an infinite amount of shit, that sounds so bad.

When I was about to go to bed that night, Mom came in to tuck me in. She doesn't always do that now that I'm big, but maybe because it was the last night she did.

"Mom, I'm afraid Hugo will be awful without you," I said.

"I'll bet he will," she said, sighing.

"Couldn't you take him, somehow?"

"And leave you alone with your darling daddy?"

I hated the way she said that, sort of sarcastically. "No! That's not what I meant!"

Mom shook her head. "I'm sorry, Nell . . . I'm worried about it too. But it's the best we could come up with. Let's play it by ear. Daddy's going to need a lot of help from you."

Lying in bed, I still felt angry about Mom's remark about "your darling daddy." It's true, I do like Daddy best, but so what? She likes Hugo best and I never say anything about that to her. Sometimes I almost feel I hate Mom. She can just say very mean things out of the blue. Why does she do that?

The bus ride in to New York was not so bad. Mom got Hugo a huge pile of comics and he just sat and read them the whole time. Hugo can be a real terror on a bus. The last time he almost had a fit and it was one of the most embarrassing things I ever went through because I was sitting right next to him and I heard this girl behind me say, "I'd like to *kill* that child." And this lady in front of us kept turning around and rattling her bracelets in his face which didn't do any good. Finally he just stopped, but till then it was pretty bad.

Our new apartment is on the same block we've always lived in, but the building is nicer. I know Mom didn't like the old building because it had no doorman and she thought it was dangerous. Once I went to get something at the store for her and some boys began chasing me, but then they went away. This new building doesn't have a doorman either, but it has an elevator man so I guess that's the same thing. It does seem like a nicer building. What I didn't like with the other one was you had to go down this long dark corridor till you got to the elevator. In this one the elevator is right there.

Daddy opened the door to let us in. I love Daddy. I know I said that already, but I really do. He's a little too fat and has lots of curly hair like Hugo, but he's sort of big and cuddly like a teddy bear. I just leaped into his arms and hugged him a million times, even though I know I'm too big for that.

"D.D." Daddy said. That's his pet name for me—Darling Daughter. "Look at you! You grew a foot! You're gorgeous. Hi, Phyll! Hi Hughs!"

Mom always gets a sort of angry expression when she sees Daddy. "Hi, how goes it?"

"Okay. How do you like the new place?"

Mom just glanced around without even moving. "Nice."

"I think the building is better," Daddy said.

"Look, if you can afford it, fine. That's all I have to say."

"I can."

"Good."

"I'll feel safer about Nell coming home from school now," Daddy said. He handed Mom a slip of paper. "Here's the new phone number. They just put it in yesterday."

"Thanks."

"Have a cup of tea, love?"

Mom stared at him. She looked surprised, maybe

at his calling her "love." "No, thanks . . . I better go. See you Friday."

Hugo was off somewhere in the rest of the apartment. I was glad he didn't see Mom go. I guess that's what she figured too. Daddy sighed after she left. "So, puss, we're on our own."

I made a face. "Yup."

"We'll make it."

"I hope so."

"Are you hungry? Did you eat yet?"

"We stopped somewhere, but I didn't feel too hungry."

"Well, why don't I whip up some hamburgers?"

"Hugo doesn't—"

"Oh, I know all about Hugo . . . I got a whole case of Beefaroni for him."

Hugo has rather strange tastes in food. He'll only eat Beefaroni, corn on the cob, raw peas and strawberry milk. It's pretty simple to feed him, actually.

I went in to get him. He was in one of the bedrooms. "Hugo, Daddy's making us dinner . . . he's making Beefaroni for you."

"Okay," Hugo said cheerfully.

I went back inside. "He says that's fine."

Hugo trotted in after me. "Where's Mommy?"

"She went back to New Jersey."

Hugo's mouth dropped open. I knew what was coming.

"You know . . . she told you, remember? We'll see her this Friday, this coming Friday."

"I want Mommy," Hugo said angrily.

"Well, she's not here."

"I want Mommy!" Hugo screamed. His face turned bright red. If you haven't seen that many times, it might be a rather alarming sight, to see someone's face change from white to red in about one second. Daddy came running in. "I want Mommy!" Hugo was screaming over and over.

Daddy said, "Hugo, Mommy is in the country. You'll see her Friday."

"I tried all that," I said. Or rather screamed because to be heard above Hugo was not that easy.

Hugo was still screaming.

"Jesus," Daddy said. "I'd forgotten about this. Do something, Nell, will you? Stop him!"

"Stop him? How? Just tell me how." No one can stop Hugo when he has a fit. You'd think Daddy would know that.

"Well, do *something*. God, that noise is horrible. Just take him away or whatever."

I took Hugo by the hand and kind of dragged him into one of the bedrooms. "Hugo, we're having supper," I yelled. "There's Beefaroni for you if you want it. When you want it, come in." And I closed the door on him.

Daddy was in the kitchen making himself a drink from orange juice and vodka. "Whew," he said. "How can someone that size *do* that? I mean, his vocal cords must be the size of a full-grown man's."

I shrugged.

"Honey, you don't drink, do you? Too bad, it's an immense help at times like this." Daddy took a big gulp of his drink.

"I'll have a Coke, if you have one," I said.

Daddy looked in the refrigerator. "I'm afraid I don't. Listen, Nell, I put that list up over there. If you want anything special, you write it there, okay? I figure I'll do the groceries once a week. We have to start getting organized around here."

In fact, Daddy is always organized, super-organized. Mom says that's really terrible, that his whole life is planned out in lists and that it's absolutely uncreative and that's why he has an ulcer and all that. You should see Daddy's study, for instance. Most people I've seen sort of spread everything out on a desk in piles and slosh it all together. But Daddy has everything all neat with charts and signs saying: DUE—MARCH 16 or LETTERS TO BE ANSWERED. He says since he works at home that's the only way he gets anything done.

30

"I'll just have milk," I said. I could still hear Hugo screaming, even though the kitchen door was closed. "I hate to hear Hugo scream like that," I said.

"It is pretty depressing, isn't it?" Daddy said.

"He just misses Mommy, that's all."

"Sure, well, it's natural." Daddy began making hamburgers. He makes good ones, really fat and crusty on the outside. Also, he always remembers to toast the bun which Mom doesn't.

We ate in a corner of the living room where Daddy had set up the dining room table. It's the same table we've always had, even before Mom and Daddy were married the second time. I remember because when I was little, I used to pretend it was a house and hide under it.

Daddy didn't eat much. He looked tired. At the end he said, "Do my ears deceive me or has there been a diminution of sound to some extent?"

"Maybe he's stopped," I said.

"Let's go see."

We went quietly down the hall and opened the door to the bedroom. No Hugo. The room was nearly empty except for the two beds, so it was clear he wasn't there. My heart flipped. I know five year olds don't jump out windows, but I suddenly began thinking of that. In our old place we always had window guards and here there weren't any up yet. I looked in the closet. That was empty too. Daddy and I looked at each other. I could see from Daddy's face he was scared too.

Then suddenly Daddy went into the bathroom and a second later peeked out and whispered, "Look at this."

I peeked in. There in the bath tub, with a pillow under his head, was Hugo, sound asleep, breathing in this loud heavy way he has, his thumb jammed in his mouth.

"What should we do?" I whispered.

"Let's put him on one of the beds . . . I can

carry him, if you can just get that pillow under his head."

But somehow Hugo held onto the pillow, even though he was still asleep. As Daddy put him on the bed, I saw one of Hugo's eyes open, but it just dropped back again. He does that and doesn't even wake up.

After that Daddy and I had dessert. I had ice cream and Daddy just had black coffee, which is the way he likes it.

"Where is my room?" I asked.

"Oh, in there," Daddy said. "I didn't really have a chance to arrange everything. I figured we could do that tomorrow."

"In where?"

"Where Hugo is. I put your bed against the wall."

"But then where will he be?"

"What do you mean?"

"Where will Hugo's room be?"

"You'll share that one."

I stared at Daddy, horrified. I couldn't believe it. "Share a room with *Hugo*?"

"Well, love, there are only two bedrooms."

"But I'm twelve years old! He's just a baby. He's not even the same sex as me."

Daddy looked annoyed. "Frankly, I didn't think the difference in sex would play that immense a role with you."

"But he wets his *bed*, he's so *little*. . . . I can't share a room with him! How will I do homework or anything? That's terrible!"

Daddy rubbed his hand over his eyes. "Listen, Nell, let's get a few things straight. We had to move because our other building wasn't safe. This one is and as a result it's a hell of a lot more expensive. We just plain can't afford a three-bedroom apartment and that's it. Now don't give me a lot of flak. I'm exhausted, I happen—which your mother in her inimitable fashion overlooked—to have moved all our stuff in here, unpacked everything, put down the rugs and books and lamps and I just can't take another tantrum. If you're twelve, act it."

I was silent. This was the worst thing I ever heard of. "You're not even paying alimony," I said, "so how come you don't have any money?"

Daddy laughed. "How do you know that?"

"I heard Greta and Mom talking about it one night."

"Well, you heard right, sweetheart, I'm not. But that doesn't mean we are now living high off the hog. I just don't earn that much. We live well, we live very, very nicely, but we are not rich. And I hope it's not that damn school of yours which gives you the idea that everyone can just float off the street and buy a five-story brownstone like snapping their fingers. There are those that can and your school is loaded with them. We are not in that elite group. I like to think we have a lot of things people like that don't have—like brains, for one. But let's face it, we'll have to tighten our belts. Hugo'll be ready for first grade next year, the whole schmeer."

I sighed. It's true the school I go to, St. Agatha's, is a school mostly for rich girls. That's just because the tuition is so high. I've always had a scholarship, so I guess we don't pay that much, but there are a lot of rich girls. Even though we wear uniforms, you can still tell underneath who has expensive things. And you can tell by where they go on vacations and over the summer and all that. I know it's awful to say, but I wish we *were* rich. Would it be so bad? Why couldn't Daddy be a stockbroker or one of those things? He might like it and still be smart and then we wouldn't always worry about money all the time the way we seem to.

"Puss, you know, it's laughable, really," Daddy said. "If you lived anywhere else in the country but New York City, you'd see that the way we live is incredibly nice. It's only in New York City that an income of twenty thousand a year is poverty level. That's just crazy."

"So, why do we live here?"

"Because I love it. And I think you do too, don't you?"

"Ya, I do, really . . . I just wish we could have everything."

Daddy laughed. "Well, frankly, I'm glad you don't—because little girls that grow up with everything are god-awful snobs nine tenths of the time. Maybe you'll be a god-awful snob anyway, but I'm still hoping for something better than that." He got up and patted my hair. "Sweetheart, be good, okay? We'll figure a way."

He went in to do the dishes while I wandered around the apartment, looking at it. It was really nice in lots of ways. The living room was big and looked out on the park. The kitchen was nicer than our last one. There was even a maid's room in the back for Daddy's study just like in our other place, and he'd set his typewriter up and his teak box for carbon paper and his black pencil holder.

"I just got an inspiration," he said, coming after me.

"What?"

"How's this? First, let's get Willi to partition your room. Build a wall halfway across, so at least you'll be a little separate from Hugo." Willi used to be Daddy's college roommate. He is a bachelor and comes to visit sometimes. He is good at carpentry and things like that.

"It's still the same room," I muttered, knowing I was being awful, but unable to stop.

"Well, listen to the rest of my scheme. It's brilliant. From the time you come home from school till the time you go to sleep—nine, ten, whatever—you can use my study as a place to do homework. I realize it's not a great room to entertain friends, but you can go in the living room for that. This will just be a quiet place if you want to get off by your-

34

self. There's even a bath here, incidentally, which may not be huge, but. . . . So, how does that strike you?"

"That would be great," I said quietly. I could hardly believe it. To be able to use Daddy's study as my own room!

"But one thing," Daddy said, wagging a finger at me, "if a single paper is messed up, finito. You get slaughtered and there is no recall. Understand?"

I nodded.

"You can use my typewriter, carbon paper, anything, but leave everything else—my work—alone."

"Sure, Daddy."

He smiled. "Well, at least we got something accomplished."

I was so tired that night I went to sleep right after dinner. But I felt so good about the idea of working in Daddy's study! Daddy does have an odd way of working. He gets up every morning at four and works from four to noon. He says he's never done a stitch of work after twelve noon in his life and never intends to. What I can't understand is actually waking up every day at four in the morning—because he doesn't even set an alarm or anything, that's just when he naturally wakes up. And he doesn't go to bed that early, usually around eleven or so. It must be great to need that little sleep, though Mom says Daddy's metabolism must be completely screwed up. He says it's just a nice time to work because everything is so quiet and dark and he feels he's getting a head start on the rest of the world.

Chapter Five

School started this morning. Every morning on my way to school, I drop Hugo off at his kindergarten around the corner from where we live. Then I take the Central Park West bus to Sixty-fifth and the crosstown across. I don't mind the ride. In fact, I like it. Sometimes I can get a seat, but otherwise I just look at the people who are usually fairly interesting.

At the Sixty-fifth crosstown stop I try to meet Heather, but we don't always plan it just right. But we always go home together after school.

Heather knows about my living with Daddy now, but I haven't told most of the other kids. I figure it's not really their business. The ones I like, I'll tell, if it comes up, I guess.

We only had half-days of school till Thursday, then we started the regular schedule. I went to Heather's house Thursday afternoon. It was the first time I'd been there since the summer.

I guess I shouldn't complain about lack of room because Heather has always shared a room. She has four sisters, two older ones in high school, Sharon and Deirdre, and Gwenn and Erin who are six and seven. Their house is always kind of noisy, but cheerful. The amazing thing about Heather's family is they are all beautiful. Every single one of them has been modeling since they were babies practically. They all have great pink-and-white skin and really beautiful red hair. (Heather's is more sort of golden red.) They all have tiny noses, the kind where if you drew them you would just make two black dots for nostrils because that's all there is. *And* huge blue eyes and long eyelashes. You'd think—I mean in books, girls who look like Heather are usually awful, sort of mean or snobbish, but the odd thing about Heather is she doesn't seem to even know she's pretty! She doesn't care about clothes, just wears jeans and shirts and when people stare at her on the street she doesn't seem to care about it. Maybe if you're that pretty, you just never have to think about it. I've known Heather since I was six, and I've seen her with the measles and after she's been crying, and once I even set her hair on fire by mistake when we were playing with candles around Christmas time, and she still always looked great.

The other odd thing about Heather is she won't model. She did as a baby and has tons of money stowed away for college and all that, but when she was around eight she just said she didn't like it and wouldn't do it any more. Her family kind of flipped out and couldn't believe it, especially because her two older sisters are crazy about modeling. But when Heather says something in her quiet, firm way, people just listen to her, and she hasn't modeled ever since then. I think her family thinks she's a little crazy and she, I know, thinks they're a little crazy.

When we got to her house, Heather's mother was measuring something on Deirdre. That's another thing—they all sew their own clothes.

"Hi, Nell, darling!" Heather's mother rushed over and gave me a big hug. Heather says hers is a very huggy kind of family. I sort of like it, maybe because my family isn't. They're all chatterboxes too, which I don't mind either, though Heather says it's just babble and she feels like she's living in a monkey house. I guess the thing is, I always feel like I consider everything I say before I say it, except with people I know well, and her whole family just seems to say anything—even if it's silly or dumb, it doesn't seem to bother them.

"Hi, Mrs. McCormmach," I said.

"You look *darling!* Look at her, Deirdre! You've grown! Goodness, look at her figure. Gosh, you and Heather are really—"

"Mom, we'll be inside," Heather said. "Okay?" She always interrupts her mother or else she says she'd never have any free time.

"Is it awful sleeping in the same room as Hugo?" Heather said. We went into her room which she shares with Deirdre and Sharon.

"Not *so* bad," I said. "He kind of snores, but I've gotten used to it."

Heather laughed.

"I like living with Daddy," I said.

"Does he cook?"

"Kind of . . . he does it three times a week and I do it three times, only we have a rule—neither of us can make the same thing more than once a week. Oh, mostly we just have hamburgers and stuff like that."

"Your mother was such a great cook!"

"I know. Sometimes I lie there just imagining stuffed cabbage. . . . But we go out weekends pretty often. And Hugo is better. In the beginning he was awful. It was just 'Mommy, mommy, mommy' all the time."

"Poor kid."

"I wish he could stay with her, but Greta says she doesn't have a maternal instinct."

"Hmm."

Deirdre waltzed in wearing a peasanty dress with

a low neckline. "How do you like, kiddos? Give me your frank and honest opinion."

Naturally she looked lovely, but Heather just grunted and said, "Quite nice."

"I like it," I said. It must be strange to be that grown-up and that pretty and still be a regular person living at home with your parents.

Suddenly Deirdre clapped her hand over her mouth. "Nell!"

"What?" She had me scared.

"What happened to your nose?"

"My nose?" I felt it to make sure it was still there.

"It looks . . . so big, sort of. Was it always like that?"

"Deirdre, for heaven's sake," Heather said.

Deirdre blushed. "No, I just meant. . . . You know, having a big nose isn't so bad. You can have them done. This girl we work with, Georgina, had a *gigantic* nose—practically like Pinocchio, and now she's the hottest model they have, she's a dream."

"She just has a big gaping hole in the middle of her face," Heather muttered.

"Oh, listen, Nell, no seriously, your nose isn't so big—it just looked kind of—looked different to me. Maybe it's just that you're sunburned or something. I just never noticed it before. But if you ever do want to—"

"Deirdre, will you stop babbling and leave us alone?" Heather said.

"Oh fool! Was I awful?" Deirdre hugged me. "Listen, everyone in our family is a blabbermouth, Nell, darling. You know that."

"That's the understatement of the year," Heather said.

"Your nose is really darling. I mean, the main thing is—does a nose go with your face? And yours does, it really does. It's just, like, if you ever did feel you wanted to have it done or whatever I do know this great man who could—"

39

Heather was just giving Deirdre a cold stare and she finally backed out of the room.

"I wish they had an operation where they could tape her mouth up," Heather said. She shook her head. "Talk about families!"

I went over and looked in the mirror. Actually, I had never given much thought to my nose before. I wonder why. Maybe it's that everyone in my family has fairly big noses, not huge, but not little tiny nostrilly ones like Heather's family either. Also, none of us are that great looking anyway. I mean, Hugo is cute and Mom can look pretty, but not in the way that you'd suggest they model for bread ads on TV or anything. "You know, it is kind of huge," I said thoughtfully. "Isn't that odd that I never noticed it before."

"Oh no!" Heather said. She was sitting cross-legged on the floor, going through her new school notebooks.

"What?"

"I wish that idiot would learn to keep her mouth shut. Your nose is great."

"But, listen, seriously Heath—is it huge? Maybe I should—"

"Look at all these people like Barbra Streisand," Heather said. "Yours is a peanut compared to theirs."

"Ya, but they sing."

"So, you—do something else. Look, I could see if you had your heart set on being a model or something, but I thought you had more brains than that."

I sighed. "Do I? I hope so."

"You hope so?" she said. "I mean, you only have the best grades in the whole class."

"Except for Wilhelmina Prensky," I said. Wilhelmina Prensky is this thin quiet girl who writes down everything any teacher says. It's weird. I once sat next to her and this teacher, Mr. Belsinger, was making a joke and she wrote it down word for word and then put in parentheses: "joke." "Anyway, I have to get good grades to keep my scholarship," I said. "I'm just a plodder."

"You wouldn't *have* a scholarship if you weren't smart." Heather glanced out the door. "Who wants to look like *her*, anyway?"

"Who—Deirdre? But she's beautiful." Of course, to Heather who's beautiful too, maybe Deirdre just looks the way a regular person would look to me.

"Oh, I hate the way she goes around waving her boobs at everyone."

"What do you mean?" It was a funny idea—Deirdre shaking her breasts in someone's face like someone shaking a dustmop out the window.

"Like—wearing that kind of dress. We all know she has them."

"Ya, I guess you're right." I sat down and began silently going over my notebook. Now that we're in eighth grade we have some choices about what we can take. I picked earth science instead of physics because I love dinosaurs and I heard it's a little about that. Heather, who is great at math and science, picked physics. Heather is better than me in this way. If she doesn't like a subject, she just won't even study for it. So her grades are all mishmashed—some A's and even some C's and D's. I just could never let myself get a D. I remember last year we had algebra which I hated but I studied and studied—or rather memorized and memorized —and I ended up getting the highest grade on the final of anybody in the class. But that seems so cowardly. I'd rather be like Heather.

"You know what a nose operation is called?" Heather said suddenly.

"What?"

"A rhinoplasty."

I laughed. "That sounds like an operation a rhino would have to have his horn removed."

Heather looked at me gravely, her head to one side. "You know, Nell, I wasn't going to mention

41

this, but now that you've brought it up, have you ever thought of having that horn removed? I mean, it is kind of noticeable just sticking out in the middle of your forehead like that."

"But I *love* my horn," I said, falling in with her.

"I know you do, it's beautiful, but, well, maybe you should stop always tying a ribbon around it to match your shirt. It looks a little too planned, do you know what I mean?"

Heather's eyes were twinkling. I love her, she's great. I'm glad she's my friend. I even forgive her for being beautiful.

Chapter Six

It seems to be working out all right with Daddy. He picks Hugo up at nursery school at one and takes him to the park in the afternoon. He says there are some other fathers, though mostly mothers, and anyway, the weather is nice—it's October— and it's nice just to sit there. A few times after Hugo and I came home from a weekend with Mom and Greta there was a big fuss again, sort of like that first time, but just knowing it's coming or might be makes it not quite so bad.

Daddy did have Willi build a partition for Hugo's and my room. It goes about three-quarters of the way across the room so you can still pass back and forth. Hugo has the side near the window, mine is near the door since I go to bed later.

What I really love, though, is being able to work in Daddy's study. I hope when I grow up, whatever I decide to be, I'll have a study just like his. I even like that it's so small. It makes me feel like I'm in the cabin of a ship with the one little window. Or else in some tiny house in the woods where everything is in one room. There's a radio and a phonograph, everything! I like taking baths there too. I guess I should feel ashamed to admit it, but I still have imaginary animals that I think about and play with when I take a bath. When I was little, six or eight, I had about a dozen. I used to always take them along and talk to them—in my head—whenever I was alone. Mom said it was because I was an only child for so long and only children do that. She was an only child too so I guess she knows. Anyway, now, when I take a bath in the little room off Daddy's study, I pretend some of those creatures—Whitey the Goat and Percival the Parrot—live in that bathroom and wait all day for me to come in there. Sometimes I sit in my bath half an hour, playing with them.

Hugo still wets his bed. Not always, but pretty often. Daddy tries to hold him back on drinking too much apple juice after six in the evening, but unfortunately Hugo is a big drinker, especially of juice.

It smells kind of putrid and awful in his room, or his half of our room, even though Daddy changes the bed. Sometimes he says it's too much laundry so he just lets the sheets dry, and by the end of the week when they've been peed on about five times, it's pretty bad. Luckily, I only go in there to sleep and I usually fall asleep right away.

One night I woke up because I heard Hugo yelling, "Get away! You can't get me!" over and over. I woke up right away. Sometimes he talks in his sleep but this time it sounded even worse than usual. I went out in the living room to get Daddy. My clock said eleven-thirty, so I guess I had only been asleep about two hours. It felt like the middle of the night, though.

Daddy was in the living room with Arden. She was sitting on the couch, looking at a book and holding some drink in her hand, and Daddy was standing near the window, as though he'd been in the middle of saying something.

"Daddy, Hugo's having a nightmare, I think," I said. "Hi, Arden."

"I'll go right in," Daddy said.

Arden is this friend of my mother's. Or anyway, she used to be—I don't think Mom likes her too much anymore, but I don't know if that's because Daddy does or what. She's married, but I guess maybe she doesn't like her husband because she does go out on real dates with Daddy, I know. She's very tiny and pretty with short curly dark hair and black eyes. Mostly, she is very quiet and hardly ever speaks. When she does, it's so soft, you can hardly hear what she is saying. When Daddy left the room, she just sat there, looking at her drink and didn't say anything. Finally I said, "Hugo misses Mom."

Arden just nodded. Then, after a second, she said in this almost whispery voice she has, "I'm scared witless of babies."

At first I wasn't sure if she said witless or shitless. I guess it doesn't matter but Arden isn't the type to use the word shit, so I guess it wasn't that. I had never thought of someone being scared of a baby before. I mean, I know some people don't like them, but why be scared of them?

"A baby could kill you," she said, looking at me seriously. "I read that once. If a baby was as big as a grownup, it would just kill . . . because it has no moral sense."

I didn't exactly know what to say. "Well, I guess it's lucky they aren't that big," I said. "Anyway, Hugo isn't really a baby," I added. "He's five."

For some reason that made her smile as though I'd said something amazing. "Is he really? God, that's incredible. I remember so well that summer when Hugo was a few months old. It seems like yesterday."

I remember that summer too. We had a house on Cape Cod and Arden and her husband, Mitchell, had a house nearby. They all used to play tennis together, and I got stuck with sitting next to Hugo's basket and seeing he didn't choke or whatever babies that age might do.

45

"How *is* Phyllis?" Arden said.

"Mom?"

"I guess she still has that job, doesn't she? You know, I admire your mother so much, Nelda. If only I had that drive! I'm such a putterer . . . I do this and that and a million tiny things. She's really committed to what she does."

It was hard to tell if she thought that was good or bad. "Ya, well, she does like it," I said, "only Greta doesn't have a maternal instinct. That's why they can't take Hugo at least till he's in school all day."

"Who's Greta?"

"Mom's friend. It's her parents' house . . . but they retired to Florida to play bridge. It's not Greta's real mother. She died of T.B. when she was little— I mean when Greta was little. But her Daddy got married again and then they went to Florida."

"I see," Arden said.

"Mom says Florida is a god-awful place," I said, "so I don't know . . . but Greta's stepmother and father like it. They play shuffleboard and things like that."

"Umm, how nice." Arden smiled at me. I wasn't sure she was listening.

Just then Hugo came padding down the hall with Daddy behind him. I guess Daddy had changed him because he smelled not so bad. Hugo is very genial when he gets up in the middle of the night. I suspect that when he grows up, he may be a night person like Daddy. "Hi," he said to Arden with a big, friendly grin, though I'm sure he didn't know who she was.

"Is *this* Hugo?" Arden said. "Oh God, I can't *believe* it. It's just impossible, Jake—he was this tiny thing in a basket about one minute ago."

Daddy shook his head. "Yup, well . . . here he is."

Hugo raced over, climbed in a chair and got down the box of chocolates Grandma Rose sent us years ago. He shoved the box at Arden. "Want one?"

"Why Hugo, how sweet. Sure, goodness, they all look so good, how can I pick?"

Meanwhile Hugo popped a few in his own mouth. "I want juice," he announced, munching.

Daddy sighed. "Okay, but just a little, Hugh . . . because, you know, we don't want another major flooding." He went into the kitchen.

"He does it while he's asleep so it's hard to stop him," I said to Arden.

She looked at me blankly.

"Pee," I said. "Hugo, I mean . . . that's why we can't give him too much juice."

She smiled and patted Hugo on the head the way people always do. "What curls! Isn't it unfair? Boys always seem to get them."

"To wash his hair you have to sit on him," I said. "It sounds cruel, but it's the only way."

Daddy brought the juice for Hugo who drank it in about one gulp. "Okay, well, listen kids, it is a little on the late side, past midnight, in fact. So, maybe you'd better—"

Arden jumped up. "Jake, darling, I better . . . I think it's getting late for me too."

"I'll go down and get you a cab," Daddy said. "Back to bed, kids. I mean it."

Hugo went back to bed. He sang to himself for about fifteen minutes, not real songs just chanting kind of singing and then suddenly he must have fallen asleep because it was quiet.

One thing I know: I hope Daddy does not marry Arden. Of course, she's married already so that is one good thing. And, I should think her husband would mind if she just went and married someone else. Though I guess she would tell him first. But I don't think I'd want a mother that just puttered around all the time the way she does. She reminds me of a child, almost, being scared of so many things. I remember she's also scared of elevators and high places and swimming. That's worse than most children! A grownup shouldn't be like that.

Chapter Seven

When we were out with Mom and Greta for Halloween weekend I told Mom about Arden.

"That idiot," Mom snorted. "Is she still drinking?"

"I don't know," I said. What I really don't know is: how can you tell if someone drinks too much? Arden is always very quiet and I thought drunk people made a lot of noise.

"Well, Daddy will be a very rich Daddy if he marries old Arden," Mom said. She was sitting in the rocker while Greta made supper.

"How come?"

"Because she is loaded and I mean loaded."

"But she said she just putters around."

"She can afford to. . . . No, it's her father. Her husband, Mitchell, poor creep, he's an accountant. But her father owns all the cleaning products in America, you know, one of these things where no matter what happens to the rest of the economy, he stays floating."

I thought of the way Arden looked. She didn't look especially rich. "Her clothes aren't that fancy," I said.

"Oh, she plays it down . . . when she wants to,"

Mom said, "but I'm sure Daddy is not, as they say, unaware of the family fortune he'd come into through her."

"But Daddy has enough money," I said. I thought that was so mean of Mom, to even *think* Daddy would marry someone just so he could be rich.

"Nobody ever has enough money," Greta said, coming in with dinner.

"But *you* always say you don't care about money," I reminded her.

"Don't listen to me, then," Greta said. "Of course I care. Look, if I didn't have my parents' house and a nice little income from their investments, I'd have to go out and get a nine-to-five job, which would be the ruin of me. It's nice to have enough money so you can forget about it."

We all sat down at the table. Hugo, who had already eaten, was playing with a train on the floor and softly chanting, "Money, money, money. . . ."

"A prophet for our time," Greta said. She looked at Mom. "Is this Arden really insanely rich?"

Mom ripped off a chunk of hot bread. "Well, insanely is a little . . . ya, sure, she *is* insanely rich, why beat around the bush?"

I began thinking—then if Daddy married Arden, I would be insanely rich too, like those people Daddy said who can just buy five-story brownstones like snapping their fingers. I don't know if I'd especially like a five-story brownstone, but maybe some other things might be nice. Like an Old English sheepdog. I always wanted one, but Mom and Daddy said just to feed it would be horribly expensive. Only I don't know if I would like having Arden around all the time, even if she is very quiet. "She never talks," I said.

"Who?" Greta said.

"Arden."

"Insanely rich Arden?" Greta said. "Well, I guess she doesn't have to. If you're that rich, you can just sit there wrapped in hundred-dollar bills and smile."

I laughed. I imagined Arden wrapped up in dollar bills. "Greta, don't be so silly," I said.

"Why not?" said Greta. "Grownups have a perfect right to be silly if they like."

"They don't," I said, teasing her. "They should be serious."

Greta made a face at me. "Blah!"

After supper Hugo and I got into our costumes. Actually, it was the first time I'd ever done trick or treating not in New York. In the city it's different since you always go just in the apartment house you live in. You go from floor to floor and if there are about three apartments to a floor, you can go to a lot of places in a very little while. Of course, some people don't open their doors because they're scared you might be a mugger in disguise.

Hugo was a ghost which was what he wanted. But Greta let me as a special treat dress up in some costumes that were in her parents' attic. I was an old-fashioned lady with a big black hat, sort of like a fancy witch. I had a black eye cover. Mom said she'd drive us around.

"But where?" Greta said. "I don't know the neighborhood that well." Greta's parents just moved here when she was in college, that was why.

"I'll just find a string of houses somewhere along the road," Mom said.

"You mean, just go into anyone's house?" said Greta.

"Sure, why not?" said Mom.

"But what if there are all sorts of weird little ladies who put poisoned pennies in apples and that kind of thing?" Greta said.

Mom looked at her and laughed. "Greta! Come on! Don't be paranoid. You've been reading too many Gothic novels."

"No, Mom, it was in the paper, it really was," I said. "There are people like that."

Mom said, "Maybe a few, but what are the chances of running into one on a single evening?"

When we set off, at seven-thirty, it was dark but not too cold. Mom drove toward Hopewell, which is the nearest town. When we went along one road, suddenly there were a whole lot of children in costumes roaming around so Mom figured that was a good place.

Everyone was very friendly, more than in New York. They all seemed to have little piles of warm cookies all ready and wrapped up and several of them patted Hugo on the head and said what a cute little ghost he was. Actually, we had a sort of disaster toward the end. Hugo had so much stuff in his bag that it broke and a lot spilled out on the ground. I thought he would have a real fit, but oddly he didn't. Mom said he was too glassy-eyed to know what was happening at that point, so we just scooped up as much as we could and drove home.

When we got home, Hugo said he wanted to sit by the door with his candy to give to anyone who would come to *our* house for trick or treat. Mom said she wasn't sure anyone would since we're way off the road and that it was getting late, but Hugo said he wanted to in a way that meant if you didn't let him there'd be a monster tantrum. So Mom let him. He just sat there for about half an hour with his bag of candy right beside him. One group of kids finally came and he gave them all a lot of stuff. But no one came after that and Mom finally lugged him off to bed.

I spread my candy out and divided it into the kind I like, such as almond joys and butter-scotch candies, and the kind I don't like—jelly beans and licorice. Greta took a stick of licorice and began to chew on it. "Maybe it's poisoned," I said, smiling.

"Somehow, with licorice, I think it would be harder," Greta said. "The papers never say anything about poisoned licorice."

I yawned. "Maybe I'll go to sleep too," I said.

Mom and Greta never make me go to bed at any special time, but I usually get sleepy around nine-thirty.

I didn't even feel like taking a bath because I felt so sleepy I was afraid I would fall asleep in the bath. As I was going up the stairs, I ran into Mom. "Are you sleepy already, Nell?" she said.

I nodded.

She came up after me. "Let me just fix up your bed a little."

She fixed it up while I got into my pajamas.

"Mom, do you think my nose is extremely big?" I said.

"Your *what?*"

"My nose. Heather's sister, Deirdre, you know the oldest one, said she thought I should have it done—you know, cut some of it off."

"Oh honey, you can't be serious. That family is a bunch of idiots, you know that."

"But they *are* very pretty," I said.

"Look at Greta's nose," Mom said.

I thought of Greta's nose, but I couldn't remember exactly what it looked like. I went downstairs. Greta was on the couch, reading. She looked up. "I think Phyllis is upstairs," she said.

"No, I just wanted to . . ." I said.

"Hmm?"

"I wanted to look at your nose," I said, feeling embarrassed.

"Look away. Is there any special purpose in this investigation?"

I touched my nose. "Someone said mine was too big."

Greta looked at me. "It is, isn't it? Well, so's mine. Somehow, there are greater tragedies in life, Nell."

"But I could have part of it cut off."

"What for?"

I thought a minute. "I guess so people would want to . . . well, take you out on dates and that kind of thing, or marry you, even."

"Well, frankly, I never *was* the belle of the ball," Greta said, "but I don't think my nose played a very large part in that. I mean, would you want someone to marry you just because he liked your nose? I would think that would be sort of demeaning."

"Not *because* of your nose. . . ." The trouble is, I guess when you're grown-up, you don't care any more. But when you're my age, you do and it's hard to explain that. I'd like to think boys will just like me because of my terrific personality or something like that, but then I'm not sure I have such a terrific personality. I am sort of shy. Well, anyway, I guess I don't have to decide right away.

Mom leaned down the stairwell. "Are you *still* looking at Greta's nose?" she said.

"Well, it's such a beauty," Greta said, "she couldn't tear her eyes away."

I went upstairs and Mom tucked me in. "Nell, you're pretty—you're not beautiful, but you are pretty. And to be beautiful is like being insanely rich. It has its own problems. I just wouldn't fret about it."

"Sure," I said.

She kissed me. "Your nose is exactly like Daddy's," she said.

Lying in the dark, I thought about that. It's true Daddy does have a big nose, but I never think of it, the way when someone asked me if he wore glasses I couldn't remember. I guess if you look at someone every day, all the time, you forget those things. So maybe if I ever get married, someone will forget about my nose. Or maybe their nose will be even bigger.

Chapter Eight

Every Thanksgiving we go to visit Grandma Rose
in Boston. She doesn't actually have Thanksgiving
dinner at her house. She only did that when Grandpa Ben was alive, but this friend of Mom's, Eliza
Lipkowitz, usually invites all of us. Only this year,
of course, Daddy won't come. Maybe he'll have
Thanksgiving dinner with Arden and Mitchell.
When I asked him, though, he said he might just
forget the whole thing.

We drove there. Mom has a red Volkswagen
which is a little crowded, but it's okay. Mom is sort
of a demon on the road and it makes me nervous
to drive with her. She drives very fast and likes to
pass people. She always mutters things to people
on the road, like—to this nun—"Okay, Sister, we
know you have to get to that retreat in a hurry, but
could you move over a little?" I try not to look
when Mom is driving, just to think things and not
notice. Hugo really doesn't notice. Anyway, he's
reached the age where he likes riddles and he
spent the whole time asking us riddles from this set
of Dixie riddle cups Mom bought for him.

"When is a black dog most likely to enter the house?" he asked me.

"When the door is open," I said.

Hugo got mad. "You're not supposed to know—you peeked!"

"I didn't peek . . . but that's just like the one about the chicken crossing the road, it's the same basic principle."

Hugo hates it if you guess the right answer. But it's sort of exhausting to listen to nine million riddles one after the other. I had a headache by the time we got to Grandma Rose's house.

Grandma Rose lives in a real two-story house, which is where she always lived with Grandpa Ben when he was alive. Mom thought she might want to move to someplace smaller but she said she didn't. What she does is rent one of the rooms to someone. Now she has a couple living with her, they're married, Natalie and Seymour Farash. She wrote us about it; we had never met them. But when we arrived, this man came out with Grandma Rose, so Mom said, "You must be Seymour," and he said he was.

He was short with a mustache and he was wearing a brown turtleneck sweater and sneakers and looked friendly. Grandma Rose is tiny with silver hair. Mom says it's blue which is not really true. Sometimes she has it dyed and it looks sort of blue, but not a real blue like a blue sky. She wears very pretty dresses, usually with flowers on them and high heels. Mom says it's an insane vanity to wear high heels, especially when they're not even in fashion anymore, but Grandma Rose says she has great legs and she might as well show them.

"I'm really glad to meet you," Seymour Farash said. "Hi, Hugo, how was your trip?"

"What is the best butter in the world?" Hugo said.

Seymour Farash looked puzzled.

"It's a riddle," I explained.

"Oh . . . well, gee, I don't know. . . . What *is* the best butter in the world?" Seymour asked.

"A goat!" Hugo yelled and raced into the house.

"He likes to tell a lot of riddles," I said. I just thought Seymour should be prepared.

Grandma Rose gave me a hug. "So, how's my beautiful girl?" she said. Grandma Rose really does think I'm beautiful—I guess grandmas always do.

"I'm fine, Granny."

Natalie Farash was inside the house, in the kitchen, cooking. She was quite fat. It's funny someone being that fat and being married. I mean, Grandma said they were newlyweds so they must just be married a little while. She wasn't just what you'd call plump like a lot of people, she was really fat. "Hi, there," she called. "I'm Nat. Do you like lentil soup?"

"I'm Nell," I said. "I don't know."

"It's going to be great," she said. "I throw in everything but the kitchen sink." She had really pretty blue eyes and long brown hair loose almost to her behind.

"Can you sit on your hair?" I asked.

"If I'm in the mood," she said, tossing some hot dogs in a big pot.

That first night, the night before Thanksgiving, we just ate at Grandma Rose's with Seymour and Natalie. It seems they don't pay Grandma rent, but they help her cook and clean. "They're angels," Grandma Rose said when I was in her room before supper. "I just adore them."

"She is a little bit fat," I said in a low voice, even though the door was closed.

"Yes, poor darling," Grandma said. "She just loves to eat. She can't stop. She's a picker, they're the worst—you know, never let anything go to waste. But they simply adore each other. I've never seen a couple so much in love!"

That's funny. Seymour seemed nice, but you wouldn't think of him and Natalie as being the most romantic couple you'd ever met in your whole life, especially if you'd lived sixty-five years like Grandma Rose.

"They've saved my life," Grandma Rose said. "They are so much fun, they just cheer me up. I just *love* them, both of them." Grandma began squirting perfume on herself. Mom says Grandma wears enough perfume to sink a ship and that you can smell her halfway to New York City. I like her smell. It's lily of the valley; that's her birth flower. She squirted some at me. "You're getting old enough for perfume," she said. "Do you use that bath set I sent you?"

Grandma Rose sent me a bath set with scented crystals to put in. "Yes, I loved it," I said. "I think I almost used it all up."

"Well, I'll get you another," she said. "A good scented bath is worth all the tea in China in my opinion."

We didn't have wine at dinner, just water. The thing is, Mom says Grandma Rose is an alcoholic, but she doesn't seem to be. Mom says she means that Grandma Rose can't hold her liquor, and when she has too much she gets mean and wild and starts to shout. I never saw that. In fact, I can't even imagine it, but I don't think Mom would make it up. Mom also says *she* can't hold liquor herself. Now that I think is true, because I do remember a few times Mom had too much to drink and she did become odd, just talking a lot and acting funny. I didn't like it at all; it was sort of scary, in fact. When Daddy drinks, he acts just the same as he usually does, even when he has almost a whole bottle of wine, which he sometimes does when a friend is over for dinner.

After dinner Natalie Farash played the guitar. She knows millions of folk songs. We all sang, except Grandma who didn't know the words. Hugo didn't know the words either, but he pretended he did.

Natalie had a beautiful voice, sort of soft and high. You almost forgot how fat she was when she was singing. Her voice sounded like the voice of a really thin person.

"I hope Eliza isn't going to too much trouble for us," Grandma said.

"Oh, she enjoys it," Mom said.

"I'll bet Arlo is just dying to see Nelda again," Grandma Rose said, beaming at me. "It seems to me—"

I turned red. I used to be good friends with Arlo when we lived in Boston. He's a year and a half older than me and he has two brothers, Andrei and Ivan who are fifteen and seventeen. The thing is, we just haven't seen each other that much except on Thanksgiving or when his family comes to New York, so for all I know he has a girl friend. Anyway, I hate it when Grandma Rose makes a big thing out of it.

"Eliza is really loving her job," Mom said, I think to rescue me from Grandma. "She's teaching at Radcliffe," she explained to Seymour and Natalie. "She's really a remarkable person, you have to meet her. She has multiple sclerosis and she's in a wheelchair, but she got her doctorate in three years and has tons of energy.

"Jesus, I wish I could get mine in three," Seymour said. He and Natalie are studying history at Boston University.

We sang some more. Mom sang her Function Junction song. This is how it goes:

> *Are you from Function? From Function*
> *Junction?*
> *Where the Function Junction suction cups*
> *are made?*

*Are you from Function? From Function
    Junction?
Well, I'm from Function toooo! Hey!*

It's sort of a silly song. Mom says she and some
friends made it up when she was at camp years
ago. They called their bunk Function Junction.

"I don't think I really understand that song,"
Grandma Rose said when Mom had finished. "Does
it mean something?"

"Not really," Mom said.

"It's sort of like a tongue twister," I said to
Grandma.

"Oh yes," Grandma said. "I never understand
those either."

Natalie yawned and then clapped her hand over
her mouth. "I hate to be a party pooper," she said,
"but I just. . . ."

"Nat needs about ten hours sleep every night,"
Seymour said, almost as though he was boasting.

"Twelve if I can get it," Natalie said.

"Which she seldom can," Seymour added.

"Daddy only needs five," I said. "He gets up at
four in the morning."

"Does he still do that?" Grandma Rose said.
"Goodness. Can that be good for his health?"

"He says he likes the feeling of getting a head
start on the rest of the world," I said.

Mom was just looking at me. So were Seymour
and Natalie. I don't know if they know I'm living
with Daddy. "It doesn't bother me," I said, "because
I just get up at the regular time, like seven, and
take Hugo to school. Daddy says if anyone talks to
him before twelve noon, he'll have them beheaded."

"*You* met Jake," Grandma Rose suddenly said to
Seymour and Natalie. "Remember over the Fourth
of July weekend . . . he was the man I went out to
dinner with that evening."

"We thought it was your secret lover," Natalie
said.

59

Grandma chuckled. "Jake is good-looking, isn't he?"

"Do you think so, Grandma?" I said. "I think he's a little too fat." Then I blushed because I remembered that Natalie was much fatter than Daddy.

"Why did Jake come to Boston?" Mom asked. She looked annoyed.

"Oh, I don't know." Grandma Rose looked flustered. "I guess he had some business or . . . I really don't know. I thought it was sweet of him to look me up," she said.

"Darling," Mom said, sort of grimly. She walked out of the room.

We all heard her go upstairs. In a whisper Grandma Rose said to all of us, "Oh dear, did I put my foot in my mouth? I *did* think it was sweet . . . I like Jake."

"I think we better all turn in," Seymour said.

"Do you think your mother is mad at me?" Grandma whispered to me in the kitchen. "I'm a fool. I shouldn't have mentioned him."

"You didn't say anything bad, Grandma," I said. I began peeling a banana for a bedtime snack.

"I didn't think I did . . . but, you know, sometimes things just slip out. I guess she's still sensitive."

I went upstairs and got ready for bed. Hugo and I share a room, but he was sound asleep. Mom's door was shut. I went out and rapped lightly on Grandma's door. "Grandma, you don't have any Tampax, do you? I forgot to bring any, and I think I might be about to get my period—I have a sort of crampy feeling."

"Oh dear!" Grandma said. "Do you get your period already, Nell? That makes me feel about a million years old. No, darling, I don't. I don't even use that stuff anymore. Maybe Natalie does."

"Oh, that's okay," I said. "I'll get some in the morning."

"We can drive around to Maxwell's," Grandma

said. She kissed me. Her cheeks are very smooth and soft, like a new pillowcase. "Sleep tight, sweetheart."

"You too, Grandma."

In the morning Grandma and I drove to the shopping center and I bought some Tampax at the drugstore. It was the only store opened. Luckily, my cramps weren't so bad. I did have a little bit of a headache so I took two aspirin. It was Thanksgiving Day and maybe I was nervous that we were going to go to the Lipkowitzes. Mr. Lipkowitz picked us up at four. I wore this new pants suit I got in the fall. I like it. It's sort of like a dress with pants, only the material is the same, brown and gold tweed. I feel more comfortable in pants. Somehow in a dress I'm always wondering if the top of my pantyhose shows and that kind of thing.

The Lipkowitzes live in a big house, about as big as Grandma's, but different. Because Mrs. Lipkowitz is in a wheelchair, their house is all on one level so she can go from room to room. It's a very nice house, modern, with lots of plants and a big piano and interesting things like a white table with white chairs around it on top of an orange rug.

Everyone in the Lipkowitz family is tall, except for Mrs. Lipkowitz and Arlo. Mr. Lipkowitz is about six feet four. Andrei is seventeen and just dropped out of college. Ivan is fifteen and wants to be a doctor, like his father. When we came in, I saw Arlo in the kitchen. He looked taller. We were always about the same height, but I haven't grown much in the last year and he'd grown quite a lot. He has shaggy dark-blond hair and wire-rimmed glasses, and he talks slowly because he used to have a stutter when he was little.

My heart was beating when he came over to say hello. It's awful to be like that. I hate myself for it. "Hi," I said.

"Hi, Nell," he said. "Mom made that stuffing you like."

Mrs. Lipkowitz always makes this great stuffing which she says is "highly unorthodox." It has raisins and apples and cornbread and chestnuts and it's fantastic. I like it better than the turkey usually. The whole house smelled so good my mouth started to water. The grownups had drinks, and Arlo and I just sat by the fire. He said he was doing a lot of photography and was developing his own prints. "Maybe I'll show them to you later," he said.

"What do you take pictures of?" I asked. I felt warm in my pants suit, especially around my neck because the collar is high.

"Oh, just people I see on buses and stuff. I took some up at Cape Cod just of scenes, but I like people better."

"Do you develop them at home?"

"I could . . . I wish I could have a darkroom all set up, but there is one at school, so mostly I do it there."

Arlo knows about my living with Daddy since Mom writes to Eliza. "Is that working out okay?" he said.

"Ya, it's. . . ." I suddenly felt like telling Arlo about Arden just to get his opinion, but Mom was right near by, so I just said, "Sure, it's working out really well."

Dinner took a long time. Eliza makes everything herself, even squash soup—which sounds awful but was very good—and her own whole-wheat bread and cranberry sauce. Grandma said, "I just feel I should starve all year before this meal, Eliza. I don't know how you do it."

"I have to admit, I was going to forget the bread this year," Mrs. Lipkowitz said, "but then I figured —oh well." She wheeled into the kitchen to get a fresh serving plate. Her wheelchair is electric and when she moves you hear a buzzing sound. I remember when I was younger it used to scare me a little.

For dessert there were two pies. You could

choose or have a piece of each. Grandma said, "I'm going to just make a hog of myself and have both . . . I'll starve tomorrow."

"Well, you're looking very well, Rose," Mr. Lipkowitz said.

"I think I'm in pretty good shape," Grandma said, "given my advanced age. I'm a senior citizen now, you know—I was sixty-five this October."

"It's hard to believe," Eliza said. "You seem to have so much pep."

"Too much," Grandma said. "That's my trouble. Well, I have to tell you this one story because it tickled me so . . . I have this meat man at the A and P. He always saves me the best cuts, marvelous prime ribs. Well, last week he said to me, 'Rose, I want to make you an offer.' He said he'd set me up in an apartment and visit me and bring me steaks twice a week. He said it right in front of everyone! Goodness!"

"With the cost of meat as it is now, I should think that's better than Chanel Number Five and roses," Eliza said.

"You may be right," said Grandma. "Anyway, I figured it's the last proposition I'm likely to get."

"You never can tell," Mr. Lipkowitz said. He put his hands on his wife's shoulders. "Why are you so beautiful, Eliza?" he said softly. "It's not fair that you're so beautiful."

Mrs. Lipkowitz blushed. "Enough flattery," she said. "Help me with the coffee."

After dinner it was dark out, really evening. Eliza started to play the piano and Mom was talking to Mr. Lipkowitz. Andrei took Hugo outside to play kickball, and Ivan said he had to go out and meet some friends. Arlo asked if I wanted to go see his photographs. I said yes.

He has his own room. It's always been the same ever since they moved here when he was six. He has a sword collection and on the wall are a lot of really beautiful old swords. On the bulletin board over his bed were a lot of photos in different sizes tacked up. He rummaged around in the closet and got out a big stack of them. I sat on the bed and began looking at them. There were some really nice ones—one especially—of this very old lady just sitting looking at the camera. She had a sad but a very nice face. "Who was she?" I asked.

"Oh, she was . . . I went into a bar and she was serving drinks," he said. "I asked if I could take her picture."

"I'd never have the courage to do that," I said.

"I didn't either, but . . . I just did it." He grinned. "Sometimes people really mind if I even aim the camera at them—Mom and Dad won't let me take them at all."

I began wondering if Arlo has a girl friend. It's not that I want to be his girl friend, but I would hate it if he was dating. But he goes to a co-ed school so he might be. I didn't see any pictures of girls in the photos anyway, but that doesn't really prove anything.

"My father has this girl friend," I said. "Her name is Arden. I think you met her that time we all had houses near Cape Cod."

"I don't remember," Arlo said. "Do you like her?"

"Not really. Mom says she's extremely rich."

"It must be strange to have your father dating someone," he said.

"Well, your parents are different," I said. "They really seem to love each other."

"I know," he said. He was looking at the window. "I almost think they love each other too much. If anything ever happened to one of them, I don't know how the other one would manage."

Arlo doesn't know how lucky he is to have parents like that. "I love it when your father tells your mother how beautiful she is," I said. I always notice that.

Arlo said, "He does that all the time."

"That's so great," I said. It made me feel sad just to think of it.

"Didn't your father . . . even when your parents were married?"

"No. At least not that I can remember." Sitting there I suddenly had the feeling I had to change my Tampax. I think the worst thing that could happen would be this thing Heather once described where she had dinner at someone's house and when she got up, she saw she'd dripped blood on the dining room chair. And it was some pale yellow very fancy chair. She said she mostly managed to rub it out with a paper towel. "I have to go . . . I'll be back in a minute," I said.

I raced into the bathroom. Luckily I had brought a huge stack of Tampax in my bag. I put a new Tampax in and went to the mirror to see if my face looked very greasy. My nose gets extremely shiny sometimes if I'm hot. I wiped it off, it wasn't so bad. Just then the door opened and Arlo walked in. Seeing me, he turned bright red and said, "Oh, I didn't know—I—" and walked out.

I hadn't even locked the door! Imagine if he'd walked in when I was putting my Tampax in!

I felt so embarrassed when I went back to his room. He was looking at some book and pretending it hadn't happened. It seemed so quiet in the room. I felt this feeling as though I had a heart in my ears and it was beating. Suddenly I took a sword off the wall and got into fencing position. "*En garde!*" I said.

Arlo took up another sword and we pretended to fence. I don't really know how, I've just seen it in movies.

"I'm going to take fencing next year," Arlo said.
"Then you'd better watch out."

"I wish we had it at our school," I said.

Then I felt better that we'd joked around. We stayed in his room awhile longer, but it was okay.

I think we both felt more at ease and just talked about school and things like that.

The only bad part was when we came out. All the grownups—Mom, Arlo's parents and Grandma —were sitting around the fire, listening to a record. Hugo had fallen asleep and was lying with his head in Mom's lap, sort of snoring peacefully.

"Well, there you are!" Grandma said. "We were wondering what had become of you two!"

Arlo turned red again. I could have killed Grandma. First of all, it occurred to me that they all probably thought we had been making out or something and here we hadn't even done anything. It's not that I would want to, but I hope the reason Arlo doesn't try to kiss me is because it's something he doesn't do that much, rather than just because he doesn't like me or think I'm pretty. What would be awful was if he just thought of me like some younger sister and really liked some girl in his class or took her to dances. I pray something like that isn't true.

Mom stood up, "I really think we ought to be going," she said.

"Well, listen, I mean it, we are coming to New York," Mrs. Lipkowitz said. "So, let's count on it. If you see a good opera in *The Times*, get tickets and we'll reimburse you."

"Don Gio—vanni!" Mr. Lipkowitz sang in this very deep voice. He loves opera too.

Mr. Lipkowitz drove us home. Grandma sat in front next to him, and Mom sat in the back with me and Hugo who was still sleeping.

It was quite dark and cold out. I rolled up my window. Mr. Lipkowitz said, "So, what has Rebecca Ingersoll been up to of late, Phyllis? We never got to her."

"Well, Greta and I are into a third one," Mom said.

"Is Greta the woman you're living with?"

"Right."

"You know, it amazes me," Grandma said, "to see a young person without a job. I think it's so wrong of parents to allow that!"

"What young person do you mean?" Mom said.

"This—Greta. I mean, from what Phyllis has said," she said to Mr. Lipkowitz, "she just stays home, lives in this house her parents have left her and—"

"Writes novels—a really filthy thing to do," Mom said angrily.

"You said she just does that in the evening."

"What the hell difference is it to you when she does it?" Mom said.

"I wouldn't have a person like that in my house," Grandma said in a loud voice, as though Mom were very far away. "They think they can get away with anything these days. It's a shame, it makes me *sick*."

Mom was holding my arm and squeezing it so tight it hurt.

"Well, I think everyone has their—" Mr. Lipkowitz began.

"If they're in their teens and finding themselves or whatever, all right," Grandma said, "but thirty some years old and still just—"

"You've never even met her!" Mom said. Her voice was shaking.

"I don't have to . . . I'm sure she's a splendid girl," Grandma said sarcastically. "You wouldn't be living with her if she weren't would you?"

We were home. Mom scooped Hugo up in her arms. "Stay with me, honey," she whispered to me. "Please."

As soon as we got into the house there were Seymour and Natalie Farash. They were just sitting in the living room, but as soon as they saw us, Seymour leaped up. "Look at you!" he cried.

We all looked at each other.

"You look gorgeous! Look at them, Nat. Grandma Rose, that's fantastic, that dress."

Grandma blushed. "Do you like it, Seymour? I like bright colors, but some say at my age—"

"You look fan*tas*tic. Listen, Rose, would you mind terribly if I took your picture?"

"He just got this new Polaroid Instamatic," Natalie said. "It takes color."

"Just sit right there," Seymour said, sort of pushing Grandma onto the end of this wing chair she has. "Okay . . . great."

"Oh dear, are you sure?" Grandma said. "Shouldn't I powder my nose?" She reached up and touched her hair. "Is my hair all right?"

Seymour was squatting on the living room floor looking into his camera. "That's it, Rosie. Terrific. Just a little to the right, toward me . . . now cross your legs, okay? We've got to get a shot of those gorgeous gams."

After he had taken a few of Grandma in the wing chair, Seymour said to me, "Now how about the two of you together?"

Grandma gave me a hug. "Next to Nell, I'll look like an old hag," she said, "but I don't care."

"Nonsense!" said Seymour. "I was just noticing how much alike you two look. It's amazing. Don't you think, Nat?"

"Definitely," Natalie said. She was nibbling on a dried fig.

"How about Mom?" I said, looking around. Then I realized she had disappeared upstairs with Hugo.

The pictures came out right away. In one of them I was blinking so it didn't look too good, but one with Grandma and me, her hand on my shoulder, was nice. "Rose Red and Rose . . . Golden Brown," Seymour said because of our dresses.

Grandma seemed all excited. "Let's have a nightcap!" she said. "What do you say? I wish I could take a picture of the two of you," she said. "I just don't understand cameras, that's my problem."

"Oh, I'm awful in photos," Natalie said. "I look

like an old hippo." She said it very genially, as though it didn't bother her that much.

Grandma had something called crème de menthe which tasted exactly like peppermint gum. It didn't have that awful burning taste most drinks do. I just had a little. Then, without meaning to, I gave this tremendous yawn. "Run on up, darling," Grandma said, "you've had a big day."

As I went upstairs, I heard Grandma say, "Now I know I shouldn't boast, but isn't little Nell the sweetest person you've ever seen? I just can't get over her, how she's. . . ."

I guess that's just the way grandmas are, there's nothing you can do about it. But it's sort of funny her calling me little Nell when I'm about three inches taller than she is!

Hugo was sound asleep in his bed. I got into my pajamas and went into the bathroom. There was Mom on the toilet, just sitting there. When she saw me, she went into a fit of giggles. Every time she started to speak, she'd giggle again.

"Mom, come on, pull yourself together," I said. "What's so funny anyway?"

"I love . . . Seymour Farash," Mom gasped, clutching her sides.

"You *love* Seymour Farash?"

"I adore him . . . I adore her . . . I'm going to leave both of them every cent I have in my will. God, they saved my life! Nell, you don't know, she was about to go off on a real screamer-dreamer. Oh, that couple. What darlings! I wonder, did they know or did they just—"

"I think they just kind of like Grandma," I said.

"Bless them. If there's a heaven, may they rise up to whatever is the best level and stay there forever with their wonderful Polaroid camera." Mom was subsiding by now. "Oh honey!"

"Mom."

"She just scares me when she gets like that. I

don't mind her drinking, but I hate her when she's drunk."

"She's having crème de menthe," I said. "I had some too. Can you get drunk on that?"

"Sure. You can get drunk on cough medicine," Mom said.

"You *can?*"

"Sure. Grandpa Ben used to go around absolutely swilling the stuff all winter long on the grounds that it was good for his larynx. Euh, what a family!"

"I hope I won't be like that," I said, squeezing some toothpaste out.

"I don't think you have the right personality," Mom said.

"How can you tell?"

"I can't really." She got up, flushed the toilet and began washing her face with soap. "I love Mommy," she said, "it's not that, but she still treats me like a child and it gets me so mad. She won't let go. What business is it of hers who I live with or how I lead my life?" She looked suddenly sad. "Don't let me do that with you, Nell, hang on like that."

"I won't."

"Promise you'll tell me if you think I am."

"Sure."

"The trouble is I guess if your own mother does one thing, then maybe you don't do that thing but you do something else, just as bad. You can't win." She splashed cold water on her face. "Holidays are something I've never been able to cope with," she said.

It's funny that Mom calls Grandma "Mommy."

Chapter Nine

I wish our school was co-ed. It seems like it's practically the only school in the whole city that isn't. All the other ones that used to be are changing except us, and the headmistress, Arabella Borchardt, says she won't even hear of it. She says that girls don't study as well with boys around and that "there's time enough for all of that when you're in college." Though I know she likes women's colleges better too. I guess by "all of that" she means sex. The thing is, I just feel I don't know how to act with boys because I hardly ever see them. How will I learn? Next year we'll have dances and mixers, and it sounds so awful, just being all shoved in some room with boys you hardly know. Heather says she's not even going to go to them. But she can say that, knowing that if she did, every boy there would probably fall on his face trying to dance with her. But how about me? Daddy says I should consider myself terribly lucky, that I'm getting a "first rate education," more than he ever did as a boy. But Daddy turned out all right, so I wonder what difference it makes.

Maybe it was seeing Arlo that made me think of

it again. I know Mom and Daddy wouldn't let me transfer to another school for high school. They say they feel so grateful to St. Agatha's for having given me a scholarship and all that. I guess it was nice of them. Oh well.

Heather is sleeping over at my house this Friday. She hasn't yet, even though we talked about it a lot, mostly because I went away to Mom and Greta's on weekends. But this weekend Mom said she and Greta will be very busy with the first draft of the third Rebecca Ingersoll, so Hugo and I are staying with Daddy. Mom did say there are a lot of new Rebecca Ingersoll letters she's been saving for me which I can answer when I go up there again.

Heather likes my room. Now that it's partitioned it's really small, but Daddy said we could sleep in the living room which has doors that close it off. That way Hugo can't pester us in the morning. Because, despite the partition, every morning at seven Hugo comes creeping around to my side of the room. Sometimes he just sits at the end of my bed with a big pile of books. But somehow he always manages to wake me up. I've tried pretending I'm asleep, but if I even open one eye, he sees it and then the jig is up. Actually, he's getting better about playing by himself. He does this funny thing. He makes up names for everyone in a book. Like if there are twenty tigers, he'll point to each one in turn, saying, "That's Jasie and that's Waylo and that's Peter and that's . . ."

This day we were lucky. Daddy had Hugo out in the park so we went in the living room and did our homework, just to get it out of the way. Daddy got home at five thirty and fixed Hugo's bath. He takes a bath with about eighty boats and rubber animals. While Hugo was in there, Daddy came into the kitchen. "Did you girls eat yet?" he said.

"We're having hot dogs," I said, "and french fries. We bought them on the way home."

"Okay."

"Daddy, should we move the beds now or after Hugo is in?"

Daddy was looking for something in the refrigerator. "What? What beds?"

"Well, I thought Heather could sleep on the folding bed and I could use the couch."

"What are you talking about, Nell?"

"Daddy! Heather's sleeping over tonight. It's all planned. I wrote it on the calendar about eight hundred years ago . . . and we're sleeping in the living room because otherwise Hugo will wake us up early."

"Well, for tonight that's impossible," Daddy said curtly.

I stared at him. "Why?"

"Arden's coming for dinner. I'm sorry, Nell, I haven't the faintest recollection of your telling me about Heather. She can stay, that's fine, but you'll have to sleep in your room."

"But we can't! We'll be all squashed together! There's hardly even room for one bed much less two."

"Daddy!" Hugo yelled from his tub.

"That's the most unfair thing I ever *heard* of," I said angrily. "We've been planning it forever."

"Well, you're a very lucky girl if your knowledge of injustice is that limited," Daddy said. He went in to Hugo.

I felt so angry. If I hadn't told him, it would be one thing. But I did. I can even remember the time I did and his saying it was okay and everything. What's awful is Daddy being so cold sometimes. Mom is bad in that she'll be unfair and yell and scream, but at least you feel she cares. But Daddy, sometimes, is so cold and detached, as though he didn't care if you lived or died. That's the worst thing for me. Especially when he can also be so nice and warm and funny.

"Nell, listen, I don't care," Heather said. "So

we'll sleep in your room—it doesn't matter that much."

"But I've been planning it so much. How can he just forget like that?" And suddenly, much to my own surprise in a way, I burst into tears. I felt so ashamed, doing that, but Heather was very nice. She just kept patting me on the shoulder and saying it was going to be all right. Finally I stopped and laughed. "I guess it's silly to make such a big fuss," I said, sniffing.

"Well, frankly, in a family of five kids, you never get that much privacy anyway," Heather said, "so I'm used to it."

Heather and I went into the kitchen and made our hot dogs and french fries. We'd bought a giant bottle of Coke, and we ate in the dining room. I wanted to eat before Hugo came in, but just as we were sitting down, he raced in with just his pajama top on and Daddy running after him. Daddy grabbed him as he reached the table. "Down on the fifty-yard line," he said.

"I want to *eat!*" Hugo yelled.

"Well, get your pajama bottoms on," Daddy said. "These ladies aren't used to dining with naked men —as far as I know."

"Daddy, don't be *silly!*"

Hugo began just reaching on my plate and stuffing french fries into his mouth. He doesn't even start to chew until his whole mouth is stuffed—like a hamster. It's a pretty disgusting sight.

After we ate, Heather put on this new record, and she and Hugo danced around the room. Heather is an excellent dancer; she has a great sense of rhythm. Hugo just crashed around, looking pretty silly, but enjoying himself anyway. Daddy was in the kitchen cooking something, I guess for him and Arden. He looked in and said, "He's not exactly a young Nureyev, is he, Heather?"

Heather said, "You never can tell, Mr. Landau."

Finally Hugo went off to sleep, and Heather and

I dragged the folding bed into my side of the room. The two beds took up the whole space. Even to sit down you had to crawl over them. "Oh well," I said, "there's no place like home."

"Who's Arden?" Heather asked in a low voice.

"She's this . . . lady—woman, I guess—who he's dating." Suddenly I got an idea. "Listen, why don't we sneak out while they're eating? We can make up some excuse."

"We're hungry . . . we want a snack," Heather said.

"Right. She's coming at eight, so, like, at eight thirty or nine, we'll just kind of creep casually into the kitchen."

"Great."

At eight ten we heard the doorbell ring, but we didn't go out. The house was pretty quiet by then, but after Arden came, Daddy put some music on the phonograph. Heather wrinkled her nose. "What's he cooking? It smells good."

"Oh, shrimp creole probably. That's his specialty."

At about quarter of nine we went out. Arden was lying on the couch. She was wearing a black pants suit and there was a cane near her with a silver top. Daddy was sitting on the edge of the couch, drinking. The room was quite dark—just one lamp was on low in the corner and there were two candles lit on the table. "Hi girls," Daddy said, smiling in this way as though he knew the real reason we'd come out.

"We wanted a snack," I said. I hoped we wouldn't start giggling. When you do that, it's awful. Once Heather and I started giggling in assembly and we just couldn't stop. It wasn't even anything that funny, we just got in a giggly mood.

We went into the kitchen and got a bag of potato chips and the rest of the Coke.

"Have you met Arden, Heather?" Daddy said. "This is Arden Kassos . . . Heather McCormmach."

"Hi Heather," Arden said. "Excuse me for not being able to move. I twisted my ankle skiing is why."

"What a great cane," Heather said, picking it up.

"Yes, isn't it a beauty? It's worth having this darn thing just to be able to walk with that. It was my great grandfather's."

I looked at the head. It was three silver monkeys holding hands. "That's our family crest," Arden said. "There's some motto that goes with it, but I always forget what it is."

"No monkey business," Daddy said.

Arden laughed. "Jake . . . you wouldn't have another fresh lime by any chance? That drink was just incredible."

"Of course I have another fresh lime," Daddy said. "I have many fresh limes." He took Arden's glass and went into the kitchen.

"You know, it's been the most amazing revelation to me, having this thing with my leg," Arden said, looking up at us. "People are so cruel, I can't believe it. I was getting into this cab and I finally got all settled when the cab driver said to me, 'Get out, lady—I can't take no cripples. I don't have time.' Can you imagine?" She looked at us.

"That's odd," Heather said. "I would have thought people would be especially kind."

"So would I," Arden said, picking up some salted nuts. "Exactly. And instead it's been the precise opposite!"

There was a pause.

"Heather is a model," I said suddenly, I don't know why.

Heather kind of glared at me. "Well, I used to be," she said. "I'm not now."

"Just because she doesn't want to. The rest of her family is."

"Your skin is fantastic," Arden said. "You must be Irish."

"I am."

76

"The Irish are either a mass of freckles or they have this gorgeous pink and white skin like you. Oh, thanks, Jake."

"Well, it was nice meeting you," Heather said. To Daddy she said, "That shrimp really smells good, Mr. Landau." Heather is so poised, it's really great, sort of the opposite of me.

We snuck back to my room and began to giggle.

"What did you think of her?" I asked, delving into the potato chips.

"Phony . . . why does she whisper like that?"

"That's just her regular voice. She always talks like that."

"She probably thinks it's sexy," Heather said scornfully. She took a swig of Coke, straight from the bottle. "I guess they're sleeping together," she said.

I almost choked on the potato chips. "They *are?* How can you tell?"

"Oh, just like the way she said, 'Jake . . . blah, blah, blah,' and kind of touched his arm."

"She's just like that."

"Umm. Why? Don't you think they are?"

"I don't know. When would they? We're always here."

"Weekends, I guess, when you visit your mother."

Weekends! How awful! Right when we were away, Arden was staying here in our own house. "Ugh . . . that's awful."

"Ya, she is kind of a drag," Heather said.

"She's insanely rich."

"How insanely?"

"The kind where no matter what she does, she'll *never* have to work. She could just go out and buy a five-story brownstone like snapping her fingers."

Heather considered this. "So, if he marries her, you'll be insanely rich?" She laughed. "Then you'll have to worry about someone marrying you for your money."

I had never thought of that. "Me—an heiress?"

"I guess so. Wow! My friend, Nelda, seen attending the first night of the opera in her diaphonous white dress and—"

"Blah, blah, blah, blah. . . ."

"Do you really think so, Miss Landau? That's one of the most interesting comments I've heard on this opera."

I flung myself down on the bed. "I think it's *disgusting* he's sleeping with her . . . I hope you're wrong."

"Look, at that age they just do it . . . they're not going to just kiss each other goodnight and stuff like that."

"I guess. It just seems so sneaky, their doing it when we're not here."

"Would you rather they did it when you *were* here?"

"No!" I yelped.

Heather laughed. "It's funny . . . I don't think my parents sleep with *anyone*, not even with each other."

"How can you tell?"

"Oh, I guess I can't really. But they just kind of go their own way . . . and they have separate beds."

"Adina Mennick says her parents have separate bedrooms even."

"When I'm married," Heather said, "I would want to sleep in one very big bed. I think it would be more cosy, apart from sex."

"But what if you wanted all the covers and things like that?"

"We'd work that out." Heather snuggled under the covers.

Heather is so sure of herself, it's really great. Imagine knowing already whether you'd want to sleep in a double bed or not when you're married. I never even thought about that. Of course, I guess that's quite far off to think about now. I'm not even a teen-ager yet!

Chapter Ten

I don't know if I feel grateful to Heather for telling
me she thinks Daddy and Arden are having an
affair. I almost think I'd rather she hadn't mentioned it. First of all, maybe it's not true, but now
that I have the idea in my head, it's hard to get it
out. I guess I don't so much mind the idea that he
might be sleeping with her—though I do mind
that too—but most of all I mind that he might love
her or be in love with her. I suppose I want to think
of Daddy's loving just me since I know he doesn't
love Mom, at least not any more. I know you can
love more than one person. When Hugo was born
and I was seven, I remember how Mom said to me
that even if she loved Hugo as much as me, that
didn't mean she would love me less because love
isn't something where you have just so much in
you and then there's no more left and not enough
to go around. Still, Arden just isn't that nice; I
can't imagine someone like Daddy caring that
much for her, I just can't.

I kept thinking of it off and on all through De-
cember. First of all, Daddy announced that for
Christmas he and Arden were going to Jamica for

a week, and Hugo and I would go stay with Mom and Greta. I didn't like that a bit. I mean, I don't mind staying with Greta and Mom—I think Christmas in the country would be nice—but I don't like the idea of Daddy and Arden going off together. I even wondered if she was paying for it since she's so rich and that made it even worse.

One night I just couldn't get to sleep. I kept falling asleep and having little snatches of dreams, then waking up and that went on a lot of times until finally at eleven thirty I got up and decided to have a snack. Sometimes a snack will make me feel more sleepy.

Daddy was sitting at the kitchen table in his blue bathrobe. He likes to have snacks too, which I guess he shouldn't if he wants to lose weight. He was having what he calls the high cholesterol special, which is a bowl of Grapenuts in a big orange soup bowl with a whole container of heavy cream poured over it and some sugar on top.

"Hi love," he said when he saw me. "Hungry?"

"I can't get to sleep," I said. "I thought I should have a snack. Isn't that very fattening?"

"It is, unspeakably," Daddy said with his mouth half full, "but it's good for my immortal soul."

"Oh Daddy!" Actually, I once tasted it and it's so rich it made me sort of queasy. Daddy always says it's because of his Jewish genes—his mother was Jewish—that he likes terribly rich things. Like his favorite dessert, which Mom used to make, is something called trifle where you soak lady fingers in whipped cream and sherry and strawberries.

I decided just to have a navel orange with honey. Greta taught me a very good way to have it. You separate all the sections very carefully and spread them out like a flower. Then you pour honey in the middle and dip each section in the honey. It's good because the orange is sort of sharp and the honey is sweet. Only I made kind of a mess of the sections like I usually do, so it wasn't as pretty as it can be. But it tasted good.

"Daddy, do you love Arden?" I said all of a sudden. It's odd, I wasn't even planning to ask Daddy that, in fact I wasn't even thinking of it, it just sort of popped out.

Daddy held his spoon of Grapenuts in the air a minute as though thinking. Daddy looks so much like Hugo at times. Of course, his hair is quite a lot gray, mixed with blond, and his eyes are a lighter blue, but he has the same kind of round, dimply face. "I'm not sure," he said.

"Do you like her, then?"

"Yes, I'm . . . fond of her," he said thoughtfully, "more than fond, at times, I guess. She's—she's had a very hard life, Arden has."

Mom once said Daddy likes helpless women because he wants to protect them and he always made her feel helpless, even when she wasn't. I wonder if he likes to protect Arden. "What I don't understand," I said, "is how come you and Mom got married—twice, even—if you didn't love each other?"

"We did love each other," Daddy said. "We just couldn't live together."

I frowned. I'm not sure I understand that.

"Honey, listen," Daddy said. "I feel you're coming to me like I should be the Great Sage of the North and give forth with some explanation of life and love and—hell, I'm the last person on earth. . . . Seriously, I just don't *know*. I'm forty-one years old and I probably don't know a heck of a lot more than you do."

"Really?"

"Pretty much. Are you disillusioned?" He pushed away the cereal bowl. "I know you like to feel there's a rational explanation for everything, Nell. Well, there isn't. Not for many things, anyway. And it's just something you learn to live with." He patted my shoulder. "Puss—"

81

"What?"

"This is a mucky time for all of us. We just have to live through it, that's all."

"Sure . . . I wish you weren't going away over Christmas, though," I said.

"Why? Would you like to come?"

I hadn't thought of that. I had just thought of them not going.

"I thought of taking you and Hughs," Daddy said, "but then I thought—I think your mother would like you to be with her."

"Is Arden paying for your trip?" I asked.

Daddy looked angry and sort of embarrassed. "Of course not!" he said. "Who told you that?"

"No one. I just wondered."

"God damn it!" he said. He slammed the refrigerator door shut hard. "If Phyllis has been filling your ears with a lot of garbage about—"

"No, she only said Arden was very rich," I said. I had eaten all my orange and was feeling sleepy.

"It's all in investments," Daddy said.

I wasn't sure what that meant, if it meant it wasn't real money, just the kind you had to put in a bank. But I decided to go back to sleep. I felt very glad Daddy had thought of taking me and Hugo to Jamaica. Lots of girls in my school go to places like that over Christmas. I guess it might be a lot of fun.

Chapter Eleven

Greta chopped down a Christmas tree. It's really beautiful, very big and bushy, the nicest one I've ever seen. Greta likes chopping wood—she says it's the best exercise there is.

Hugo and I are going to stay out here all week. Mom has to work—she only gets Christmas day off, which is Friday. So generally she leaves at seven in the morning and Hugo and I spend the day alone with Greta.

In the morning I usually do my homework or answer a few Rebecca Ingersolls if there are any. This house has so many rooms it's easy to get off where it's quiet. Greta is good with Hugo, which is surprising since she said she didn't like little children. She lets him help her cook things and make bread. She's strict with him. She says if he wants to help, he has to be a real help and do a good job. So she has him peeling carrots and stirring things. He really seems to like it.

We all have lunch at twelve, and then Greta usually takes a walk. Sometimes she says she wants to be by herself and won't let us come along. She'll just stomp off into the woods and sometimes not come back for hours. So then I read to Hugo and play with him or sometimes take him for a little walk not too far from the house. But sometimes Greta says we can come along. She never actually says, "I want you to come," but with Greta, if she even lets you, that's something.

She knows all the walks all around. Her parents own acres of land, so you can walk for miles without reaching another house. Sometimes I've been scared we'd get lost because the snow covers all the paths, but she always knows her way back. Usually she goes back a different way from the way we came so we can see different things. If Hugo whines and says he's too tired, she just says, "Buck up, old fellow! It's good for you." She'll never carry him the way Mom would.

In the late afternoon Greta makes a fire in the fireplace. We sit in that room and read or play while she goes in to fix supper. Mom doesn't get home till nearly six and she always says, "I am starved! This winter air!"

We eat a huge dinner. I like eating well. With Daddy all we ever have is tuna fish or hamburgers, and you can get sort of sick of that. Whereas Greta makes spaghetti with thick mushroom sauce and fresh grated Parmesan cheese. I think I've gotten a little fatter already. My slacks all feel tight around the waist. But the doctor is always saying I'm too thin, so I guess he'll be glad.

After supper, when Hugo is asleep, Mom and Greta work on the new Rebecca Ingersoll. I just read or listen to the radio; they don't have a TV. I get sleepy very early—around nine—so I just go to sleep. In the country I think you get sleepier because it's so quiet and dark and cold out. You look forward to burrowing under the covers.

This year Mom wants to trim the tree herself. She says her very happiest memories of Christmas are that she used to go to her aunt and uncle's house and when she came home, her parents had trimmed the tree all by themselves and everyone would gather around and sing Christmas carols. We've never done that, but I guess this year Mom thought it would be a good idea. She said, "I'm getting sentimental in my old age." She's thirty-seven, which I guess is fairly old.

Christmas Eve after dinner I heard Mom and Greta talking in the kitchen. Mom said, "I'm not going to pull it off."

"Pull what off?" Greta said.

"Christmas, the whole bit."

"What's the whole bit? We have a gorgeous tree, nice presents."

"But I'm nervous."

"Oh, come on."

"I am, Greta, really. Holidays do that to me."

"We'll have a nice, relaxed evening trimming the tree. I'll whip up a batch of eggnog."

"I don't even know how to *make* eggnog," Mom said mournfully. "I always buy it at the store."

"Well, my father has some fantastic dark rum secreted away somewhere and this is going to be eggnog like you have never tasted in your life."

"Don't let me get drunk."

"Phyllis, *relax.*"

"I can't!"

"After a few swigs of this eggnog you won't have a care in the world."

"Will you have some too?"

"Sure."

I watched Greta as she made the eggnog. She let me taste it. Actually, I thought it tasted better before she added the rum, but I guess grownups like that sort of winey flavor.

At ten I went upstairs to sleep. I don't really get excited the way I did when I was little, but in some way I still do. Even though I don't believe in Santa Claus anymore and I know I'll probably get some of the things I want, still I like thinking about it.

Outside it's all snowy the way it should be but usually isn't in New York.

At about four or sometime very early in the morning I woke up. If I was really little, I probably would have rushed in right then to open my presents but I decided to just pee and go back to sleep till later. It was still pitch black out. Then I heard this crash in the living room.

I padded downstairs and there was Mom, still trimming the tree. The whole room was the most awful mess I've ever seen, decorations and tinsel and paper and string all spread out over everything. The tree looked quite nice, but too many of the decorations were on one side—the other side was almost bare. "Nell!" Mom whispered.

"Mom, how come you're still trimming the tree?"

"Oh honey, I'm just smashed. . . . Aren't I terrible? I'm smashed out of my cotton-picking mind and it's Christmas Eve!"

"It's Christmas *Day*," I said.

"That's even worse. Oh honey, forgive me, will you? I'm a mess!"

"I don't care, Mom," I said, "only why don't you go to sleep?"

"But Hugo—he's at that age and I wanted the tree to look perfect—but I feel so woozy I can't climb that ladder and put the star up."

"I'll put it up," I said.

"Greta's sound asleep," Mom said, pointing to her. "She just stayed up to keep me company."

I looked over at the couch. Greta was asleep. She was wearing a poncho and you just saw her face, eyes closed, and her hair all spread out on the pillow. I climbed up the ladder with the star. It's a very pretty one made of glass. I tied it as close to the top as I could reach.

"Thanks honey. You're wonderful. I love you."

"Mom, go to sleep."

"Look at this room!"

I giggled. "It *is* kind of a mess, isn't it?"

"I guess we can always clean it up in the morning," Mom said. She sighed. "I wanted to give you both such a nice old-fashioned Christmas."

"It will be."

"The presents are over there. I wanted to sort them, but I think the names are on them anyway."

"Sleep tight, Mom," I said.

"Oh, I will," Mom said. "I feel like I'll sleep till New Year's Day. Can you manage Hugo in the morning?"

"Sure," I said.

I went back to sleep, but not that much later I heard Hugo crashing down the stairs. I squinted at my watch. It was six thirty. It was still quite dark out. I decided to sleep until seven thirty if Hugo didn't wake me up.

He didn't. I even slept till eight! When I woke up, Greta and Hugo were downstairs. Greta was clearing up the mess, folding papers and things.

"Thanks for the present," Greta said. "It's beautiful, Nell."

For Greta I had made a cookbook. I wrote out recipes and drew little pictures to go with them and tied it all together with gold thread.

Mom had given Hugo a building set and he was already—I guess with Greta's help—constructing a huge house in the middle of the room. There's one unusual thing about Hugo. He's not at all greedy. When I was his age, I remember I always gave Mom a list of these toys I wanted, things I'd seen on TV mostly. But Hugo never asks for anything. And whatever he gets, he seems to like, it's odd. I got him this doll, a boy doll called Caleb with black skin and an Afro. It came with clothes but that was too expensive. Anyway, it was just lying there so maybe he won't even play with it. I might play with it. I still sort of like dolls, though I guess I'm too old for that.

For breakfast Greta made these wonderful blueberry pancakes with special blueberry syrup that she'd made herself over the summer and then put away in little jars. I ate about a dozen and Hugo ate nearly as many. "Should we save some for Mom?" I said.

"I doubt she'll make it for breakfast," Greta said. "Let's go out for a walk."

The snow was fairly deep outside—some had fallen during the night. Greta brought out fresh suet and bread crumbs for her birdhouse. It's always quite crowded. But Greta doesn't like the fact that the starlings chase away the chickadees. Greta looks funny in her snowsuit. It's a real snowsuit, sort of like a baby's, all one piece made of bright purple nylon. With it she wears a stocking cap in bright colors—red, yellow, blue, green stripes all the way to the end where there's a big pompom. And she wears these red mittens and yellow rubber boots. With the sun out she was so bright that I could hardly look at her.

First we had a snowball fight, but then Greta said she wanted to make a snow woman. She said it wasn't fair that people always make only snow men. She said we should make it in a shady place so the sun wouldn't melt it. Actually, she and Hugo mostly did the snow woman. It looked really funny when they were done. It had a big bust and a big behind, so it sort of stuck out in front and back. Greta put a straw hat on its head and gave it a cigarette and a big smile made out of raisins. It looked friendly, but sort of crazy, like some people you see in the New York subways. "Who is she?" I asked.

"My stepmother," Greta said.

"Does your stepmother really look like that?" I said.

Greta laughed. "No . . . well, maybe a little."

Meanwhile, while they were doing the snow woman, I did a snow dog. I took two carrots for his ears, which almost made him look like a small donkey, and I took two rocks for his eyes. I would have liked to go on and make a snow cat and a snow bird, but my feet were getting cold, even though I had fur-lined boots on. So we all went back inside and tried to warm up.

At one o'clock, just as we were sitting down to lunch, Mom strolled in. She was still in her bathrobe and her hair was sort of wild as though she hadn't brushed it yet. "Wow," she said. "What time is it? Is it 1974 yet?"

"It's 2074," Greta said. "You've slept a hundred years and we are the descendants of the people you knew in your former life."

Mom poured herself some juice. "I wouldn't be surprised," she said. "Listen, everyone who remembers last night, please forget it."

"I slept through it unfortunately," Greta said. "Did something exciting happen?"

"It wasn't one bit exciting," Mom said. "It's all your fault, Greta. That eggnog! Wow!"

"It was good, wasn't it?"

"It was *lethal*."

"Open your presents, Mom," I said.

Mom went into the living room. "Gee, who did all this? I can't believe it. It's so neat! Incredible."

I had opened my presents early. They were good. Mom had gotten me what I asked for—a biography of The Rolling Stones. Grandma got me this lovely jewelry box, red leather with little drawers lined in yellow silk that you can pull out. Daddy got me an amber pin shaped like a butterfly. I love it. I think even if I were terribly rich, I wouldn't like things like diamonds or emeralds. I really like amber and opals best. I put Daddy's pin on right away and wore it all day long.

While we had lunch, Mom had breakfast. She said she couldn't face split pea soup with frankfurters on an empty stomach. "Greta, I love it," she said when she opened Greta's present. Greta had bound Mom a book of sayings from the works of Virginia Woolf. She once took a course on bookbinding so she knows how. It was this really pretty paper, blue and gold. Mom sniffed and said we were all wonderful and she didn't deserve us. Hugo said he wanted to sit on Mom's lap and she let him, even though usually she says he can't while she's eating.

In the afternoon we went to a Christmas carol service at the Episcopalian church. Greta says her parents were Episcopalians and she likes their service. It was nice. Everyone sang at the end, including some unusual hymns I didn't even know. Then we all drove home and Mom made a fire in the fireplace. Greta got out her esrag and played a little for us. She spent a year in India once and studied the esrag, which is a little like a guitar. She said you really have to study it a long time to be any good.

Mom was under the tree helping Hugo build something. "This is a great tree," she said. "If you had asked me that at three yesterday morning, I don't know *what* I would have said . . . but now I really think it looks good. Did I tell you that Nell put up the star, Greta?"

"Good for you, Nell," Greta said.

"It's a little crooked," I said.

It got dark quite early and we listened to Christmas music on the radio. Greta sang some carols as she was doing the dishes with Mom. She said she had been told when she was in high school that she had a dangerous voice; they wouldn't let her join the school choir. "I was just close enough to being on tune to throw everyone else off," she said.

"Daddy has a terrible voice," I said, remembering how he used to try to sing carols. That made me think a little of him with Arden in Jamaica. I don't think I would like to spend Christmas in a warm place. I like there being snow and Christmas trees and things like that.

Hugo kept asking riddles out of his new riddle book which Mom bought for him, until finally Mom dragged him off to bed. When she got back, she sighed and said, "You know, this was the best Christmas I've ever had." After a second she added, "Maybe that's because I woke up at one in the afternoon."

"Maybe," Greta said; she winked at me.

Chapter Twelve

Daddy said he had a good time in Jamaica. He said maybe over spring vacation which is in March we can all go there. I was hoping he meant just me, Hugo and him, but probably he means Arden too. Oh well, I guess I should just get used to that.

School is good this year in that there's no teacher I hate the way I hated Miss Romaldo last year. I didn't hate the subject she taught that much—history—but what I hated was she used to do such odd things like make us fold the paper just a certain way for tests and write our answers just on the left side of the page. If you forgot, even if your answer was correct, you got zero.

In February our English teacher, Mrs. Pontoon, got pneumonia and we had this substitute, Mr. Vance. He was this middle-aged man with whitish hair and glasses. I wouldn't have minded him except he kept making remarks to me like, "Nelda of the glistening eyes . . . what do you think of this poem? You look like you must be thinking very profound thoughts." Everyone teased me afterward about it. Once after class he asked me, "Do you write poetry?" I said, "No." He said, "You should

. . . you have a poetess's eyes." I almost died I felt so embarrassed. I was really relieved when Mrs. Pontoon came back.

At the end of February Heather and I almost got into trouble. I guess we did something silly. It didn't seem really bad when we thought of it. We both had these plain white blouses that we didn't like that much, and we thought it might be fun to sew labels on them from other clothes just for decoration. Only in most of our clothes the labels had fallen out. So since Heather had to go shop for a spring coat, we decided to take a razor blade along and cut labels out of some of the dresses and coats she tried on. "They shouldn't buy things for the label anyway," Heather said. "That's just snobbish."

We went to Saks Fifth Avenue where Heather's mother has a charge account. We took about a dozen coats into the dressing room and Heather told the saleslady in this very snooty voice, "We'll bring them out when we're done." Heather can sound about thirty-five years old if she feels like it. Actually, she knew right away which coat she wanted, a plain navy blue with gold buttons, but they didn't know that. Heather stood near the curtain with one coat on, just in case the saleslady came in again. She did once, just as I was trimming a label out, but Heather just said, "I just love all of them. Maybe I'll take two, I have to think about it."

Of course, the saleslady was delighted she might be taking two and didn't come in again. Also, luckily for us, a lot of girls were there buying spring coats so they were rather busy. I cut out about a dozen labels. I did it very carefully because I didn't want to injure the material. The trouble was I was so nervous it seemed to go very slowly. Finally I just felt too nervous to do any more; we both kept giggling. Heather got her navy blue coat, and we hung all the others back again.

When we got home, we sewed the labels on our white blouses and they looked terrific. Everyone in school thought they were great. The only bad part was we told Deirdre and Sharon how we got the labels and they told Mrs. McCormmach. She went into a tailspin and said it was just terrible, exactly like stealing and we should be ashamed of ourselves.

"But we didn't *take* anything," Heather said. "We didn't hurt the coats one bit."

"I can't believe you girls would have so little sense," Mrs. McCormmach said. "This is very serious and I'm going to have to call your father, Nell."

I thought Daddy would just laugh the whole thing off, but he didn't. When I got home, he said it was a "very wrong" thing to have done. He said that if we'd been caught it would have been considered an offense which would go into our records and make it impossible to get into a good college. I got really scared. I mean, it was over and we hadn't been caught, but it's true we might have been. Also, what was stupid was we probably could have found labels at home if we wanted, if we'd really tried.

"Nell, you know, you better start using that head of yours for something other than school work," Daddy said. "I mean it. To ruin everything, all your chances, for something like this!"

"Don't tell Mom," I said.

"Of course I will. She should know."

"Please, Daddy, don't. What good will it do? We won't do it again, ever . . . I swear."

He looked at me and shook his head. "It's not this one thing. . . . You're getting to be an age where if you want, you can do a lot of foolish things that you'll regret for a long time. So stop and *think*, Nell! Please!"

"I will, Daddy! I *said* I will!"

I didn't even feel like wearing the blouse any more after that, because every time I did people would comment on it and say something like, "Where did you get such a clever idea?" Pretty clever.

I felt ashamed, as though I'd fallen out of Daddy's good graces, which for me is worse than almost anything I can think of. When Daddy gets mad, he doesn't yell and shout like Mom, but he looks so serious and speaks in this very quiet stern way which is terrible. I hate it.

But in March Daddy said that he was thinking of taking Hugo and me to Jamaica with him and Arden, if we wanted to go for our spring vacation. I felt so good, like he must have forgiven me and decided to give me another chance. Also, spring vacation is sort of nothing much, it comes so close to the end of school and in New York the weather is all gray and gloomy. I went and bought a new bathing suit. Bikinis look awful on me. Frankly, I hardly need a top yet, and I hate the idea of wearing one stuffed with all that padding. So I just got the kind I always do with shorts and a top.

"Will Arden's husband come?" I said as Daddy was packing.

Daddy just looked at me. "Honey, come on."

"Well, I thought she was still married."

"She is, technically."

I'm not sure what that means. But I decided not to ask. Anyway, I guess Daddy still likes her or feels whatever he does feel for her, since he's been seeing her all year almost. And he never sees any other women. It's hard to understand.

We flew down. Hugo loves flying. Maybe he's too young to feel scared or maybe it's just his personality, but he runs around and all the stewardesses love him and give him goldfish crackers and glasses of ginger ale. Arden was very quiet and read a copy of *Vogue*. Daddy read *The New York Times* and then closed his eyes and slept.

We are staying at a very big hotel called The Blue Moon. We have two rooms, one for Arden and Daddy, one for me and Hugo. We are across the hall from them. I think our room is almost nicer—it looks right out on the ocean. There is a wonderful sea smell in the air.

Hugo and I wake up early. We like to here because up till now we've hardly ever had a chance to be on the beach. Daddy said we can go down and have breakfast by ourselves. The dining room has a patio so we eat outside. The orange juice is great, freshly squeezed. I drink about six glasses of it a day. After breakfast we go up and change into our suits. Sometimes Daddy and Arden are ready to go out by then, but if they're not, we just go down alone. We can tell if they are ready because Daddy hangs a sign on the door, saying: COME RIGHT IN! which the hotel gave him. If the sign is not up, he says we are not to come in under any circumstances.

The beach is beautiful. The sand is white and the water is really clear. I lather Hugo up with sun cream because, like Daddy, he can burn very quickly, he has such fair skin. I'm the opposite, like Mom. I turn brown as a berry right away. Hugo isn't much of a swimmer—I think he's a little scared, though he says he's not. But he builds sand castles, and I get him seaweed and shells to decorate with.

Usually at around eleven Daddy and Arden come down. Arden has a black bathing suit, one piece. She doesn't have a really sexy figure, but it's quite good. She wears huge sunglasses, even when she goes in swimming. Her bathing cap is made of rubber petals like a flower.

Daddy usually just lies under the beach umbrella, reading. He says he doesn't like lying in the sun. He says as long as he can't tan, why should he look like a boiled lobster? I guess that's right.

For lunch sometimes we just eat on the beach and have a box lunch—hard boiled eggs and fried chicken—which you can buy from the hotel. Then we all go back to rest. Daddy says it's not good to be out in the sun all the time. Usually I wouldn't like to rest in the middle of the day, but since we get up so early I often feel sleepy and just konk out till two or even three. Then we go down again or maybe Daddy will rent a car and take us on some excursion.

It's funny—you hardly notice Arden is here. I never saw anyone talk so little. When Mom and Daddy were together, they both talked a blue streak every second. It was really noisy. That wasn't just when they were yelling at each other but when they were having a good time. They told jokes and things like that. Arden just sits there, and you can hardly see her face because of her big sunglasses. Sometimes she'll suddenly say something, but it's always a little strange, not having that much to do with what's going on, as though she'd been daydreaming. Hugo doesn't like her and I don't think she likes him. Once he took off his bathing suit on the beach because he had sand in it. I rubbed him off, but afterward she whispered, "I think people are watching us, Nelda."

I looked around. I couldn't see anyone watching us. Anyway, Hugo in the nude is not such an impressive sight that even if people did see him, they would drop everything and stare. But Arden seemed almost upset. Maybe when she's alone with Daddy, she's different. Or maybe he likes her being so quiet since Mom was not at all like that.

In the evening we all have supper together, and sometimes after dinner Daddy takes us to this place where little dogs race around a track. I don't like it. It seems cruel and I hate the idea of betting on dogs. One night Arden bet and won a lot of money. She got all excited and began to laugh. That's funny if she is so rich. You'd think she wouldn't care. I bet too because Daddy said I should, but I lost. So did Hugo.

Sometimes at night Arden and Daddy go off by themselves. Then Hugo and I stay in the lobby and play cards or just go back to our room. One time a lady adored Hugo and took us to the restaurant. She ordered piña coladas for us. Hugo kept hoping we'd meet her every night, but I guess she must have gone home because we never met her after that.

One morning after Hugo and I had breakfast, we went up to change into our suits. When we got into them, we went out to look at Daddy and Arden's room. The sign saying COME RIGHT IN! wasn't up, but the door was a little bit open, so I figured they must be up and it would be okay to go in.

Daddy was lying in bed and Arden was sitting on the window sill, smoking. She was in this very short lacy nightgown that stopped just about where her legs began. Hugo raced over and leapt on Daddy's bed the way he always does. "Heigh-ho, Silver!" he yelled and started to ride on Daddy, but Arden in about one second ran over, grabbed his arm and dragged him off the bed. "You stop that, this minute!" she said. "Your Daddy is sick! Don't you know any better?"

"He didn't know he was sick," I said. She looked so angry. Arden is very tan since she came here and looks very pretty. But I didn't like her getting that mad at Hugo who looked like he was about to let out a mighty howl.

"Why did you come in here?" she said. "The sign isn't up. I mean, Jake, if we can't even have a minimum of privacy—"

"The door was open," I said, "so we thought you must be up. It's ten thirty." I walked over to Daddy's bed and looked at him. He was lying down with the covers over him. His eyes were closed. He did look sort of pale, especially next to Arden who was so tan. "Are you okay, Daddy?" I said.

"I'm not too good, love," Daddy said.

"What's wrong with you?" I felt this cramp in my stomach which I always get when I'm nervous.

"It may be nothing," Daddy said. It made me

even more nervous that his voice was so low and he kept his eyes closed.

"At least call the doctor!" Arden said. I'd never seen her so excited.

"Arden, cool it, will you?" Daddy said.

"I've never heard of such an insane thing!" Arden said, flouncing around in her nightie. "I just can't believe it. If you don't call a doctor, I will."

"Do you hurt anywhere?" I said.

"I have some pains," Daddy said. He opened his eyes, "but they come and go . . . I did call the doctor before we left and he said not to worry about it."

"Those guys are idiots!" Arden said. "Don't tell me about doctors! They butcher anyone they can lay their hands on."

I stood there, looking at Daddy. Suddenly Hugo said, "I want to go to the beach!" I think he just wanted to get away and I can't say I blamed him.

"That might be best," Daddy said. "Maybe you and Hugo should just —"

Arden walked over and picked up the phone. "I am calling a doctor," she said, "and I don't care what—"

Then a funny thing happened. The phone was next to the bed and Daddy sat up and threw it across the room. "Get your hands off that goddamn phone," he said to Arden, "and shut up for one damn second, will you!"

I've never in my life seen Daddy so angry. I could hardly believe it. Arden just stared at him. Then she pulled off her nightie, stood there one second with nothing on, pulled on a dress and pantyhose, grabbed her pocketbook and sandals and stomped out of the room, slamming the door.

Daddy was lying back again. "Exit the queen," he said with just a trace of a smile.

I didn't know what to say.

"Love, go out on the beach," Daddy said. "We'll

decide what to do later. We might have to go back a little earlier than we'd planned, that's all."

"Do you want me to get you anything?" I said. "Some water or—"

"No thanks, sweetheart, I'll be okay. Don't worry."

"Okay, sure."

Hugo and I went out on the beach. But I couldn't think of anything except Daddy's being sick. Every time I tried to think of something else, my mind just seemed to wander back to the thought of his being sick. It was like my whole brain was just filled up with that one thought and there wasn't room for anything else. I just sat there and watched Hugo play around. Oddly the time went very fast though I didn't do anything.

At first I thought we might see Arden, that she would come out to the beach, but she didn't. Finally I said to Hugo, "I'm so worried about Daddy." I said it just because I wanted so much to talk to someone and there was no one but Hugo.

"Is he going to die?" Hugo said, but he said it in this very cheerful, calm voice and kept right on building his sand castle.

I couldn't believe it. I know Hugo loves Daddy, but maybe five is just too young to understand anything. "If he dies, we can bring flowers to his grave," Hugo said. "We can come every Sunday the way Henry Mulligan does with his grandma."

"He's not going to die," I said angrily. I felt like strangling Hugo. How can he be so insensitive? "We might have to go back to New York sooner," I said.

Hugo smiled. "Daddy threw the whole phone across the room," he said. You could tell that had made more of an impression on him than anything.

"He was mad at Arden," I said.

"I wish he hit her right in the head," Hugo said.

"Hugo, that isn't such a nice thing to say," I said, but I couldn't help smiling at the idea of it.

"Boom!" Hugo yelled. "Right in the old head!"

I sighed. Luckily the noon whistle blew and we had to go back.

"I'm hungry!" Hugo announced. "I want a piña colada."

Piña colada is this drink made of coconut milk and pineapple juice that Hugo loves. Usually I would have bought him one, but I wanted to get up and see how Daddy was. "We'll get it later."

"I'm thirsty," Hugo said. "I want it now."

"Hugo, you're almost six years old," I said. "Now stop being a baby. You can wait five minutes."

In the elevator, Hugo said, "Where's my riddle book?"

Hugo takes the riddle book Mom gave him everywhere, even to the beach. Sometimes he corners people who are sunbathing and starts asking them riddles, but sometimes he just has it there next to him.

"I don't have it," I said. "Did you leave it on the beach?"

"Yes," he said.

"Oh Hugo!"

"I need my riddle book," he said.

"You don't need it right this second. We'll go down for it later."

"Somebody might take it."

"Nobody wants your old riddle book."

"It's new," Hugo said. To the elevator operator who was on our floor he said, "I got it for Christmas."

"Well, look, go back down and get it, then. But promise me you'll come right up the minute you find it—and if it's not right where we were, don't wander all over the beach looking for it. Just come back. Because they have a Lost and Found here. Somebody might have turned it in."

"Can I have thirty-five cents for a piña colada?" Hugo said, smiling in his most winning way.

I was really ready to clobber him. "Hugo . . .

101

okay, here. But remember what I said. If you're not back here in five minutes, there'll be big, big trouble. Okay?"

Hugo was smiling at the elevator operator as though to say: how could such a cute little boy like me give anyone any trouble? Much they know.

I went down the hall to Daddy and Arden's room. The door was closed and the sign COME RIGHT IN! wasn't up, but for once I didn't even care.

The room was dark. Daddy was lying in bed. Arden didn't seem to be there. I thought he was sleeping, but he said, "Nell?"

"Umm?"

"Hi, love."

"How are you feeling, Daddy?"

"I think we're going to have to go home, hon."

"Oh . . . Okay. Do you still have those pains?"

"Off and on. I better go where we can clear up what this is. It might be nothing at all. . . . Where's Hugo?"

"He forgot his riddle book. He went down to get it." My eyes were getting used to the darkness, but I couldn't see anyone else in the room. "Where's Arden?" I said.

"She came back for her suitcase. She went back to New York," Daddy said.

"Oh."

"Love, would you do me one tremendous favor? Could you go downstairs and tell the man at the desk we're checking out after lunch. And have him phone in a reservation for us on Eastern Airlines for sometime early this afternoon."

I did that and when I got back Daddy was sitting up in bed. He had pulled up the shades, but he was still in his pajamas. "Hon, I wondered—do you think you could do me one more favor? Could you pack my stuff?"

"Sure. Where is it?"

"Well, the suitcase is in the closet. The clean clothes are in that bureau, just look in all the draw-

102

ers and whatever you see, throw in. Don't worry about how neat it is. That pile in the closet is the dirty stuff . . . put that on the other side of the suitcase. I'm sorry, love. It's not fair for you to have to do all this. It's your vacation too."

"I don't mind," I said. I didn't really. I just still had this stomach ache from the idea of Daddy's being so sick. Daddy is never sick. He never even has colds and things like that, the way most people do. Mommy always has headaches and takes pills, but Daddy never does. So that was what made me more scared.

I put all the clean clothes on one side of the suitcase and the dirty ones on the other side.

"Okay, great. I really appreciate this, Nell. The man you marry will be very lucky."

"I wonder if I'll get married," I said.

"If you want to you will," Daddy said.

Of course, that's just Daddy's opinion. I don't even know if I'll have such a big choice as he thinks. Oh well, that's pretty far away.

Hugo found his riddle book. He came into Daddy's room. "Where's the phone?" he said right away. That's all he could think of, the phone, not even how Daddy was.

"You must be really strong, Daddy," he said. After a second he added, "But you missed Arden."

Daddy laughed. "I wasn't aiming at her."

Hugo looked disappointed.

"Arden's gone home," I said to Hugo, "and we're going after lunch."

"Back to New York?"

"Yes." I had been afraid Hugo would throw a huge fit about cutting the vacation short, but he just said genially, "Okay." You never can figure out with Hugo what he'll do.

"Nell, why don't you take the brute off, clean him up and get yourself dressed, and pack and all that. We can have a bite to eat before we go."

"Are you feeling well enough to get up?" I asked.

"I think so."

Daddy still looked pale after he got dressed, but otherwise not that different. He didn't talk very much. I didn't either. I wished so much this was something I was dreaming and I could wake up. I wished I could start the day over from the time we walked into Daddy and Arden's room and Daddy was okay and nothing had happened. I couldn't even feel that good about Arden not being there. It didn't seem to matter that much.

In the plane back Daddy just slept. He had a seat by himself and Hugo and I were further up. Hugo kept wanting to go back and say something to him, but I told him he couldn't.

New York was cold and rainy, like winter almost. We got our bags and got into a cab. When we were in it, Daddy took a bill out of his wallet. "Nell, listen, here's fifty dollars. I want you to take this cab out to Mommy and Greta's house. It may cost a lot since it's so far away."

"Where will you go?"

"I'd better go to the hospital. I might as well track this thing down, whatever it may be."

"What do you think it is?"

He was silent a moment. "I don't know, love . . . I'll call you when I know."

The cab stopped at the hospital and Daddy got out with his suitcase. He hugged both of us. I tried so hard not to cry. I knew that would make him feel even worse, but after the cab drove off I just burst into tears. Hugo was very sweet. I guess he hasn't seen me cry that much. "What's wrong, Nell?" he kept saying. "Are you sick too?"

"Oh Hugo!" I just hugged him and kept on crying. I felt so silly, but I just couldn't help it.

"Daddy is okay," he said. "He got dressed."

I had to laugh, even though I was still crying. "Yes, he did get dressed, didn't he?"

The drive to New Jersey seemed to take forever. Then the cab driver got lost and said he didn't know how to find Greta's parents' house. I didn't know either. I know it's near the town of Hopewell, but I didn't know how to tell him to get there. So we stopped at a gas station in Hopewell and I called Greta and she said she could come and pick us up.

"Daddy is sick!" I told her as soon as we were all in her car.

"I know," she said.

"How do you know?"

"The hospital called."

My heart turned over. "Is he—how is he?"

"Phyllis will tell you. She spoke to them."

I wondered if Greta knew what was wrong with Daddy. Even if Mom had answered the phone, she ought to have known. Maybe it was serious, she didn't want to say anything. She just kept driving and didn't say anything like: did you have a nice trip?

Back at the house I ran right into Mom's arms. I started to cry all over again. Usually I never cry, but this one day I just couldn't help it. Mom let me sit on her lap, even though I'm too big, and hang on to her. "What does he have?" I said when I could speak.

"He had a heart attack," Mom said.

"Is that very bad?"

Mom nodded.

I thought only old people had heart attacks, people who were sixty or seventy. Daddy is only forty-one. Then I remembered how Daddy's brother had a heart attack and died five years ago, and he was only forty-seven. I hadn't thought of that because he lived in California and I hardly ever met him, so I didn't have that much reaction when it happened.

"Will he die?" I said.

"We'll keep our fingers crossed," Mom said.

That made me feel awful. I wished she would lie and just say no. I won't be able to stand it if Daddy dies. I know that has nothing to do with it, but that's the one thing I could never stand. I don't know what I would do. I don't think I'd mind being in a wheelchair the rest of my life, like Arlo's mother, or having only one arm. . . . I really don't think I would mind those things half so much.

I wished I could go back and use all those wishes that I'd wasted on new stars and things like that and give them all to the wish of Daddy's not dying. Of course, I know those things are silly, they don't control anything, but I still wished it.

"Poor Nell," Mom said.

Hugo was off under the table playing with his building set.

"You still have the Christmas tree up," I said.

"I can't bear to take it down," Mom said, "but maybe this weekend. . . . That's a good idea. It's shedding all over everything."

Chapter Thirteen

The day I went back to school after spring vacation a strange thing happened. I was standing in the hall next to Heather, waiting to go into English class, when I heard this girl I know fairly well, Posy Martin, saying to someone, "Her father died over vacation—that's why."

My heart just turned over. I suddenly thought maybe Daddy had died and no one had told me, that they had wanted to spare my feelings. Or that maybe he had just died an hour earlier and someone had called the school. Part of me knew that wasn't likely, but I just stood there, hardly able to move.

"What's wrong?" Heather said.

I didn't say anything. Heather knows about Daddy, but I still find it hard to talk about.

We found out that the girl Posy had meant was someone in a grade above ours, Kelly Ribicoff. It seems that on Easter morning she went in with her mother to wake her father up and he was dead. He had just died in bed, in his sleep.

What a weird coincidence, to have something like that happen to someone in my own school. Actually, Daddy is much better. He was in the intensive care ward for about four days, but now he is out. He can even have visitors, but I am not allowed to see him since only people over sixteen can visit. Mom hasn't gone to see him, even though she could. When she first said that she wasn't going to, I felt so angry, I really hated her. I couldn't understand. I mean, even if they are divorced if someone is that sick, you'd think you would want to see them. Because other times Mom has said that if you have ever loved someone, that person is a part of your life forever. I just couldn't understand it. We did always hear how Daddy was, though, because his friend, Willi, used to call us a couple of times a week. I felt like I loved Willi. Mom says he really is very fond of Daddy and since he's not married, maybe his friends are more of a family to him. Anyway, every time I heard his voice on the phone, I felt so happy, I wished I could kiss Willi over the phone, even though he didn't really do anything to make Daddy get better.

One odd thing is that Mom said Daddy had been having these pains for a month, but his doctor kept telling him it was nothing. By the time he got to the hospital, he had already had his heart attack. I feel so bad every time I think of him lying in bed and Arden sitting there in her nightie.

Willi says Daddy will be in the hospital for another two weeks. Then, if he keeps doing well, he can go home. But everything is going to be different now. Hugo and I can't live with him anymore. It would be too tiring, Mom said. I was hoping they would say that just Hugo would be too tiring but that I could stay, but Mom says Daddy needs absolute rest, that he may not go back to work on the same schedule; he has to try and relax. For most people I guess that would be easy, but Daddy once said he can do anything but relax. Mom said now he will have to: it is a matter of life and death.

I think of Daddy every minute. I don't think I

listen so much at school—as much as I should—but I can always borrow Heather's notes. Even now that I know Daddy is better and that he will live, I can't stop thinking about it. He is too young for it to have happened, that's what I keep thinking. It's not fair. If he was a grandfather, it would be all right. But a father should live at least until you are married.

It was so nice, this year living with Daddy, but now it will never happen again. Willi will help move our stuff out and we will live in New Jersey with Greta and Mom. Mom still has to work every day, but Greta says she will look after Hugo since his kindergarten school is almost over for the year anyway. I thought Greta would mind because of her not having a maternal instinct, but she and Hugo seem to get along very well, almost better than Hugo and Mom. Greta is more strict with him, but he really obeys her, which is something he hardly does for anyone. They go fishing together every afternoon. Greta got Hugo a straw hat just like hers and they sit on the edge of the river bank and fish for carp. Greta says Hugo really caught a fish once, but I bet she really helped him.

I drive in to school with Mom in the morning. We have to get up very early, at six thirty. Now that it's spring, it's beautiful out and I don't mind so much. I'm even getting used to Mom's driving. Mostly I try not to look. Mom says she is a good driver. She says she is fast, but not reckless, that she never gets tickets. I hope that's true. She drops me off at school and then goes on to her job. After school I go to Mom's place and we drive home at five o'clock. Sometimes I go to Heather's for a little while or to the library or, if it's really nice, I just walk down Fifth Avenue to where Mom works which is Forty-eighth and Seventh Avenue.

Her job is at a place called The Admirable Finance Corporation. It's funny to see Mom there; she seems different. She has her own desk and she wears glasses and has lots of papers in front of her. I don't really understand what she does. She's tried to explain it to me, and I usually almost understand it and then I find my mind starts wandering and I don't really know what she's talking about. At her job there are other people, mostly men, and Mom jokes around with them. I guess it's funny to think that she has this other life, the way I have school, that I never even think about. I just think of her with Hugo and me and Greta, not as an actual person with a job.

The weekend after we came home from Jamaica, Greta and I went to a movie. Mom said she was feeling run down and would baby-sit with Hugo. Seeing the movie was terrible. It was almost as bad as that day in Jamaica. It was an Ingmar Bergman movie called *Cries and Whispers*. First of all, it was gory which I absolutely hate. There was this one scene in which a man sticks a knife into his chest—he is trying to kill himself because he is mad at his wife. He goes staggering around the room with blood all over everything; it was awful. At the end, when it passed on to a new scene, Greta whispered to me, "Did he try and kill himself?"

I couldn't understand how she hadn't known what he was doing, it was so gory. But I noticed later that Greta wasn't even watching most of the movie—she had her hands up in front of her eyes. Later she told me she had read the reviews and knew when a gory part was coming, so she just didn't watch.

"Why didn't you tell *me?*" I said.

"Oh, I don't know. . . . Most people aren't as cowardly as me," Greta said.

Well, I am the worst coward that ever *lived*. If someone even jumps out at me and says boo, I almost faint. But even that part where the man put the knife in himself wasn't the worst. The worst was that the whole movie was about this woman dying. There was this one scene where she starts to gasp and can hardly breathe and I felt like running out of the theater. I didn't think I could ever forgive Greta for taking me to that movie. I almost couldn't stand it. Then, at the end, after the woman has died, there is a flashback and she is in a swing with her sisters, thinking how happy she is. Well, first of all, you know she's going to die. And also you know her sisters don't really love her, so her being so happy is fooling herself, in a way. But mostly what made me feel so bad was that I sometimes—quite often, in fact—think the way the woman did at the end: right now, at this moment, I am happy. And the movie made it seem like that wasn't a real thing to do, that she was just making up her own happiness.

As we were coming out of the theater, Greta put on these dark sunglasses right away, even before we got out. I was crying, but I said, "No fair, Greta, hiding behind dark glasses."

Greta laughed nervously. "Wow, that was a triple whammy," she said.

"So why did you take me to see it?"

"I didn't know," Greta said.

"But you said you read the reviews."

"Well, I knew it was depressing, but I didn't think it would be that bad."

I looked at the ground. I still felt angry at Greta. "I would never have seen that movie if I had known what it would be like," I said.

Greta put her hand on my shoulder. "Nell, I'm so sorry. I was an idiot." After a few minutes she said, "But don't you find it helps at all, to see a movie about something you have strong feelings about?"

I shook my head.

"I'm really sorry, then. Was it her dying that—"

"Oh just everything!" I said. Ever since Daddy has gotten better and they say he will live, I've tried not to think at all about the idea that he might die. It's like there is that thought and I just put

111

it away where I can't see it, and the movie made it come out again.

"You know," Greta said slowly, "this thing with your father. . . . Well, sometimes it's good for people to know they've been living the wrong way, then they can change."

"I want him to live a long time," I said swallowing. I was so afraid I would start to cry. "Till I'm thirty or so."

"Probably he will."

"But his brother died at forty-seven."

"That doesn't always mean anything," Greta said.

We drove back to the house. When we got home, Mom was up, working in her study. "Oh hi, folks!" she called out cheerfully. "How was the movie?"

Greta and I looked at each other and burst out laughing. It wasn't funny, really, not at all, but we just couldn't stop, even though Mom kept staring at us as though she thought we were crazy.

Chapter Fourteen

There's only a few more weeks of school. Our school ends in May. Daddy says he will rent a house this summer and Hugo and I can come and stay with him. Mom said my cousin Cynthia who is sixteen will come and stay to be a mother's helper. At first I felt insulted because I thought I was old enough to look after myself and Hugo. But then I thought how much nicer it would be to have someone else look after Hugo for a change, so I could just do things by myself. Also, Cynthia is quite nice, though actually I don't know her too well. Probably if she is sixteen, she will be interested in boys and that sort of thing.

May second Daddy came home from the hospital. Mom said I could visit him after school and she would pick me up there after work.

When I saw Daddy, I ran over and hugged him. He looked fine. I felt so glad. He was dressed and didn't even look sick at all. I could hardly stop hugging him.

"You don't even look sick!" I said.

"I feel good," Daddy said. "I lost a little weight. A

couple of weeks in the hospital is probably just what I needed."

That's like Daddy, to joke around even about something serious. He rumpled my hair. "How have you been, D.D.? You look well yourself."

"I worry about you every minute," I said. Then I thought maybe I shouldn't have said that, that he would feel worse.

"Sweetheart."

"Will you relax now and live differently?" I said, thinking of what Greta had said.

"I'll try," Daddy said. He smiled at me. "The man who didn't know how to relax," he said. "That's me. Isn't it crazy, Nell? Give me a book to do on assignment in two months and I can do it as easy as pie, but tell me to just sit around and chew the fat and I can't."

I nodded. "But now will you try to be different?" I asked anxiously.

"I will, love."

We were sitting near the window and I began looking out at the building across the street. I couldn't look at Daddy when I spoke; it was too hard. "I didn't think I could—I can't live if you don't," I said finally. "What will I do?"

Daddy sighed. "Love, you know, it's funny, I remember when I was, well, maybe a little younger than you, I felt the same way about my mother. I couldn't imagine what I would do if she ever died. But when she did, I was grown up and I had my own family and it was bad, but it wasn't as bad as I had imagined then."

"Do you promise to live until I'm grown up with my own family?" I said.

"I promise."

"I might not even *have* a family," I said.

"I think you will," Daddy said. "I hope you will."

It seems so far away, in fact impossible, to think of having my own family. I can't even imagine it.

"You're a teen-ager now," Daddy said.

It's true. I was thirteen last week, but somehow with all the worry about Daddy I didn't even think much about my birthday. "I don't feel any different," I said.

"We'll have to go out shopping for your present," Daddy said. "Some weekend, maybe."

I hesitated. "Will you be able to?"

"Sure! Look, the doctor said exercise is the best thing for me, I'm too flabby. I have to get out on the tennis court with you this summer and really get into shape."

Daddy always used to say his whole family was unathletic and there was nothing he could do about it. "What about your Jewish genes?" I said, thinking of how Daddy likes very rich foods.

"I'll have to fight it."

"What about heavy cream?"

"Ah, there's the rub. I can give up smoking, I can give up drinking, but giving up heavy cream is really cutting to the quick."

I laughed. "I love you, Daddy."

"I love you, darling."

"Hugo does too," I said slowly. "It's just he couldn't really understand. . . . That day you got sick, I was so mad at him. All he kept talking about was how you threw that phone. He couldn't think of anything else."

Daddy chuckled. "Good old Hugo. I miss him, amazingly enough."

"Have you seen Arden?"

Daddy looked right at me. "No, I don't think I will any more, actually."

"Because of what happened?"

"Because of a lot of things."

I sat there, thinking of that. A few years ago if Daddy had said that, I would have started hoping Daddy and Mom would get back together again. But now I know they won't, ever. They love each other—or did—but they can't live together. Someday I'll understand what that means, I guess.

115

Mom came at five thirty to pick me up. I think it was the first time she'd seen Daddy in a very long time, since before he was sick.

"You look well, Jake," she said.

"Isn't it strange?" Daddy said. "I feel like I've come back from a vacation."

"Did you lose weight?"

He nodded. "I want to take Nell shopping for her thirteenth birthday present one of these days," he said. "Will you lend her to me?"

"Certainly," Mom said.

I felt so good as we were driving to Hopewell. Things aren't the same, maybe they never will be, but I still felt good.

Chapter Fifteen

School is over in just one week. I'm spending the
weekend with Daddy because he wants to go shopping for my present with me. But Friday night I
am baby-sitting. It is really complicated. Heather
was the one who had this baby-sitting job to begin
with. The person or people who have this child are
some business clients of her father who are staying
at a fancy hotel, the Sherry Netherland. They are
in town for a week, and Heather's father promised
she could baby-sit for them on Friday night. But
the thing is, Heather met a boy at the Forty-sec-
ond Street library where she was doing some re-
search for a paper, and she told him she would go
out with him Friday night. So she asked me if, as a
special favor, I would baby-sit in her place. The
couple doesn't know what she looks like, so I can
just say I am Heather. I said I would do it. Heather
says they will pay two dollars and fifty cents an
hour, which is more than I've ever earned for baby-
sitting. Usually I just get a dollar and maybe car-
fare if it's far from my house.

Then, to make it even more complicated, Tues-
day Arlo called. He called me at Mom and Greta's

house. I guess Mom had been in touch with his mother so he knew where I was. He said he was coming to New York for this conference of high school editors, and he wondered if I would like to do something Friday night. He didn't actually say, "Would you like to go out on a date with me?" but I guess it's the same thing. I was so excited, I said, "Yes!" right away, and then suddenly remembered, after I'd hung up and we'd made arrangements where to meet and everything, that I had that stupid baby-sitting thing. Naturally I'd a million trillion times rather go out with Arlo than go baby-sitting. It seemed so unfair to have it happen the same night. But I'd promised Heather and she's done so many nice things for me that I felt I couldn't back down. So I called him back at this number he gave me.

"Arlo, the thing is, I forgot, I have this baby-sitting job Friday."

"Oh."

He sounded sort of disappointed. I wondered if he thought I was making it up and didn't really want to see him. "I would really like to see you," I said, "but I just can't get out of it. I'm doing it as a favor for this friend."

"Well, I guess there's nothing you can do about it, then," he said.

"No, I guess not."

There was a silence and I felt so awful I didn't know what to do.

"You know—would you like—you could do the baby-sitting thing *with* me," I said. "It's at this big hotel called the Sherry Netherland."

"Sure, that would be great," he said.

Whew! What a relief! "I think it might be just a little baby, so once it's asleep, we'll have a chance to talk and everything."

"Okay. Do you know the room number?"

I gave him the room number which Heather had given me and told him to meet me there at nine.

Actually, I was supposed to be there at eight, but I figured it would be better if he came once the couple, the Szaszes, had left. Some couples don't mind if you bring a friend, but I didn't want to take a chance. If he was there when they came home, there wouldn't be anything they could do about it.

I've hardly ever been in a big hotel. It was really fancy, even bigger than the one we stayed at in Jamaica with Daddy and Arden. Daddy was at home and I had told him where I would be. I didn't tell him about the thing of my supposedly being Heather for this evening because I didn't think it would matter. Heather and I had planned that if her mother called, I would answer and say she was in the bathroom or changing the baby or something.

The couple, the Szaszes, were the most attractive couple I've ever seen except in a movie. They were both beautiful, if you can say that about a man as well as a woman. They were both very tall with extremely gleaming black hair—his was sort of long and hers was very short. She was wearing this long white dress and he had a shocking pink jacket. They weren't the type you would imagine would have children at all.

"Heather, this is so sweet of you," Mrs. Szasz said. "Hans and I really appreciate it. We'd hate to leave Gambril with a total stranger."

I thought Heather was more or less a total stranger to them, but I guess they meant just that they knew her family. "When do you think you'll be back?" I said.

"Oh lord, I don't know. Do you, Hans?"

"Does it matter?" he said. "We don't want to be tied down. We'll put you in a cab, don't worry."

"There's a color TV in the bedroom," Mrs. Szasz said, "and if you get hungry, just ring Room Service."

"Okay," I said.

"About Gambril," Mr. Szasz said, "just do your

best. She's an angel, really, but she's sort of over-excited—she missed her nap today."

"Where is she?" I asked.

"She's in having her dinner—in there. She knows all about you. She loves sitters usually."

"What time would you like her to go to sleep?"

"Oh gosh, whenever it works out. Do your best. Not after nine, I would say. Otherwise she may be swinging from the rafters."

"Okay."

I went into the room they pointed at to find Gambril. She was sitting in bed, eating supper off a red plastic tray. "Hi!" she said cheerfully.

She was sort of a funny looking little kid. She didn't look the least bit like her parents—maybe she was adopted. She had wiry blond hair and very light eyebrows and eyelashes, so light you could hardly see them. She was sitting cross-legged, wearing a really beautiful lacy nightgown and red sneakers. I guess she was about two, but very tiny for her age. "That looks like a good supper," I said.

"ghetti," she said, pointing to it. She was making kind of a mess. The spaghetti was drooping out of her mouth and she began pretending to be a walrus with the spaghetti strands as her tusks. Then she took the canned peas in the section of her plate next to the spaghetti and just scooped them up in her hand and stuffed the whole portion into her mouth.

"Would you like a spoon?" I said, though it was kind of late for that. She just shook her head and grinned a big green mouthful.

Dessert was strawberries. They were canned too and sort of mushy from the juice. She took them one by one and began placing them on the plastic mat which was under her plate. The mat was in the shape of a cat and she put some on the ears, some on the eyes, some on the paws. Then she ate them one by one, licking her fingers when she was done.

"I want to eat the mat," she said suddenly, laughing as though this was the greatest idea ever.

"Gambril," I said, worried because it was past eight thirty and Arlo might come in any minute, "why don't I read you a story? You should be in bed soon." There was a stack of picture books scattered around the floor. I started to pick one up, but she scampered over and got two. One she handed to me. "You read *this*," she said. She took another one for herself.

"Wouldn't you like me to read to you?" I said.

She shook her head, but began looking over at my book. "This is about a little girl and her doll," I said. "See. . . ." I tried reading the text, but even though there weren't many words, Gambril got very impatient. One line she loved. "Pigeons, peck peck pecking in the park." At that her whole face lit up.

"Peck peck pecking in the park," she repeated. I guess the sound appealed to her. She pointed to one of the pigeons in the picture. "That's a yadat?" she said.

"That's a pigeon," I said. "See, he's eating those crumbs the little girl is feeding him."

Gambril pointed to another pigeon. "That's a yadat?"

"No, that's a pigeon too."

She pointed to another. "That's a yadat?"

"Gambril, these are all pigeons. Can't you see? They're birds."

She gave a big grin. "I want to *eat* the birds!" she said.

"Well, you can't. It's part of a book. And even if they were real, they wouldn't taste very good."

"I want to eat the *book!*" she yelled happily.

"Gambril, do you want me to read to you or not?"

"Read," she demanded. "Read peck peck pecking in the park."

"Well, we read that page already. Wouldn't you like me to turn the page?"

"No turn!" she said.

She must really like pigeons. Meanwhile, it was quarter to nine. "Gambril, it's getting very late. Your Mommy said you should go to sleep."

"No!"

"Look at what a nice bed you have. What pretty flowered sheets. Let's fix it up. I'll plump up the pillow for you." She was watching me with curiosity.

"Plump," she repeated.

"That's a word meaning to puff up, to . . . pounce on something." Before those words were out of my mouth, she took a flying leap and landed on the pillow. "Pounce!" she yelled.

"That's right Gambril, pounce right into bed," I said, relieved

Just then there was a knock on the door. I went to answer it. It was Arlo. He looked the same, but different. I guess what was odd was seeing him here, in New York, in this strange hotel. He had on a denim shirt and jeans and desert boots. "I'm trying to put her to bed," I whispered.

Arlo walked in with me. By then Gambril was out of bed, taking more flying leaps at the pillow, yelling, "Pounce!" very loudly.

"Gambril, this is Arlo. He's going to baby-sit with me. He's a boy."

Gambril gave Arlo a thorough once over. Then she grinned. "I want to *eat* the boy!" she announced.

"Now Gambril, I mean it—it's bed time. Right away. No more pouncing. I'm turning off the light." I took up her tray, carried it out and clicked off the light. Arlo closed the door behind me.

"Wow," I said.

"Will she go to sleep?" he said.

"I don't know. She certainly seems fairly lively."

We went into the bedroom which was the bedroom of the Szaszes. "They said we could watch the TV if we wanted," I said.

Arlo shrugged. "Well, maybe later."

I felt nervous. I wished we were doing something, going somewhere. It was awkward just sitting in the room. "Was your meeting good?" I said.

"Ya, it was really interesting," Arlo said. He began describing what it had been like. I could hear Gambril singing in the next room. She wasn't singing so much as chanting a song and she evidently didn't know the words. "Da da da da da da da! Da da da da da da!" She sounded cheerful, anyway. "Yes, that's true," I said.

Arlo looked up. "What?"

I realized my mind had been wandering. I was so nervous about Gambril not going to sleep. "Oh, I'm sorry," I said.

Arlo just looked down. I felt like I had hurt his feelings which was so stupid. "I just wish she would go to sleep," I said.

"We don't have to talk about the meeting," he said quickly. "It was sort of dull."

"No, I'd like to."

There was a pause. Then Arlo said, "I know I talk slowly . . . I just sort of trained myself to because of the stutter."

"But you don't have it any more."

"If I'm nervous I do."

"I hardly ever noticed it."

We were sitting side by side on this seat in front of the TV. All of a sudden Arlo took off his glasses and put them down on the coffee table. Then he turned and kissed me. The strange thing was it was such a long kiss. I've hardly kissed that many people, but when I have, it's always been more quick pecks and that sort of thing. But this kiss went on and on. I felt like the first time I tried to swim underwater, as though I might not come up. Finally we kind of burst apart and looked at each other and laughed.

I think it's much harder to kiss someone you've known a very long time like Arlo. We didn't know what to say. He looked different without his glasses.

123

"You must have kissed a lot of people," he said finally.

"Me?" I was going to say hardly anyone, but I thought that would sound too bad, so I said, "No, not so many."

"You seemed very experienced."

"I did?" I thought about that a minute. "I thought *you* did."

"Oh no. I almost never have done anything with anyone."

"But you go to a co-ed school."

"Oh yeah, but if you know people since you were in nursery school and see them every day, it's not that—I don't know—the girls in my class are sort of strange anyway. They're very aggressive. I mean, one of them—this girl, Meryl—she told my friend, Roger, she would do anything with me, if I wanted." Arlo turned red.

"Is she nice?" I said, hating her.

"No, she's sort of crazy, I think."

I nodded.

"Why are you staring at me?" Arlo said, but in a nice way.

I felt my face grow warm. "I didn't know I was. . . . No, maybe it's just you look different without your glasses." Really, he looked very good looking. He has lovely greenish eyes. I think if he never wore glasses, he would be too handsome.

"I'm practically blind without them," he confessed.

"Can you see me?"

He laughed. "I'm not that blind." Then he kissed me again.

I like kissing and even hugging. But the rest—well, maybe it's just I haven't done it, but the idea of it scares me. I bet once you've done it, you don't feel scared anymore. I wish you could go to sleep and wake up and find that you'd done everything and it would never be scary again after that.

Just then, while we were right in the middle of

124

kissing, the phone rang. Before I had time to stop him Arlo reached over and answered it. "Oh, you must have the wrong number," he said. "There's no one named Heather McCormmach here."

My heart sank. "Let me answer it," I whispered.

I took the phone. Of course it was Heather's mother. "Oh, hi Mrs. McCormmach!" I said.

"Hi, Nelda. Who was that who answered the phone?"

"Oh, that was just . . . this friend of mine, Arlo, who I wanted Heather to meet. His parents are friends of my parents." I thought that would sound good.

"Where is Heather?"

"Oh, she's . . . in the bathroom."

"Could I speak to her?"

"Well, the thing is—could she—um, speak to you later? We're sort of busy with the baby right now."

"But it's ten o'clock!"

"Umm, well, she . . . just woke up. I think she had kind of a bad dream and Heather is . . . she's gone to get her a drink of water."

"Oh. Well, as long as things are under control."

"Oh, they are! Everything's fine." I heaved a sigh of relief.

"Why did your friend say he didn't know anyone named Heather McCormmach."

"Oh he—he just came and . . . he thought you meant the couple. He didn't know Heather's last name."

"I see. Okay, well, give my love to the Szaszes."

"I will, Mrs. McCormmach."

When I hung up, Arlo said, "What was all *that?*"

"Oh, it's stupid. I think she suspects something." I told him all about Heather and my doing this as a favor. "Did I sound very nervous?"

He nodded.

"Darn it! I never can act differently from how I feel. I wish I were like Heather."

"Why?"

"Well, she can act anyway she feels like. She can sound thirty-five years old if she wants."

Arlo said, "I think it's good you show what you feel, Nell."

I swallowed. I wondered if he meant about kissing. I hope he couldn't tell too much that I like him. I know you're supposed to play it cool and all.

After that things were quite peaceful. We started watching this horror movie on TV but it got quite scary and we turned it off. I told Arlo about the summer, about Daddy renting a house. I was hoping he would say he could come and visit us, but he said he was going on a bicycle trip for that month.

"Is your father feeling okay?" he asked.

"Yes, he looks fine. Only it was so scary. It was terrible." I still don't even like to talk about it, even though it's over. I started to tell Arlo because his mother has been sick and I knew he would understand, but when I opened my mouth, nothing came out.

"You don't have to talk about it," Arlo said.

"I just—" Tears began rolling down my face. I felt so ashamed. "He's fine now," I whispered. "It's all over. I just—"

Arlo began patting my shoulder. "Don't feel bad, Nell."

"I don't, I won't. I'm sorry, but I love Daddy so much. If anything happened to him . . ."

"Mom said he has made an excellent recovery," Arlo said.

"He has." I felt so good that Arlo was nice about my crying. "Everything's going to be fine," I said.

"My mother's always been sick," Arlo said, "ever since I was born, so I guess I . . . for me it's just part of life."

"But do you find you just get used to it and you don't worry any more?" I said, hoping that would be true.

"Maybe, sort of," Arlo said. "Only sometimes—

126

well, I'll be in the kitchen and see how hard it is just for Mom to move around, to reach things."

"She does so much!" I said. "You'd never know she was sick, even."

"I know." He had his glasses on again and looked just like he always did. He was silent a minute, but I didn't rush in and say something the way I usually do. Arlo just talks slowly and I have to remember that and not try to finish sentences for him the way I sometimes do. "But there are times when she just has to lie down, or you can see—just by her face—that she's in pain. I can just tell, by looking at her."

"But you can't really do anything to help her?" I said.

"Not that much." He looked at me. "The worst thing, Nell, would be if she gets worse. Right now she's been the same for years and maybe she always will be. But sometimes people with M.S. suddenly get worse. Dad told me that once. That would be the worst thing because once it happens you can't stop it."

I nodded. It's funny that there are some families really who never have problems like these, and kids whose parents love each other from start to finish and never get sick. "Do you ever wish—" I began and then stopped.

"What?" Arlo said.

"Well, just that your family was just normal and regular."

Arlo smiled. I love his smile. It's very slow and gentle. "Sure," he said.

That made me feel better. Sometimes I feel guilty even just thinking that.

At one thirty the Szaszes came home. Unfortunately by a coincidence Gambril woke up about three seconds before they came in the door. She began singing that "Da da da da da da da!" song again.

"Ye Gods, is she still up?" Mrs. Szasz said.

"Oh, hi Mrs. Szasz. No, she must have just woken up. She's been fine—she went right to sleep."

Mrs. Szasz opened Gambril's door. The room was a wreck. Gambril had dragged her whole mattress onto the floor—how I don't know, considering how tiny she was. She had draped a sheet over the coffee table and made a tent, and she was stark naked. "Hi, Mommy!" she called out cheerfully, running into Mrs. Szasz's arms.

"Monkey face!" Mrs. Szasz said. "This is no time for you to be up."

I was really scared they wouldn't pay me since they would think I hadn't done a good job, but Mr. Szasz just stuffed fifteen dollars in my hand. "This is Arlo," I said. "He came to baby-sit with me."

"Hi, Arlo," Mr. Szasz said. "Hello and good-by."

"Hi," Arlo said, and we went downstairs to get a cab.

I dropped Arlo off in the cab since our house was further than the place he was staying. "I'll see you in the fall," he said, patting my shoulder. Then he leaned over and kissed me very fast, but on the lips. "I had a very good time, Nell."

I swallowed. "Me too."

Daddy was sleeping when I let myself in. Of course, probably he was soon going to get up to work. Then I wondered if he still does that since his heart attack. Maybe he doesn't anymore. I went into Hugo's and my partitioned room. It was funny to be there without Hugo, to be there as a guest sleeping over when before it had been my own house. It seemed like there was still that Hugo smell in the air which was partly his peed-on sheets and his animal crackers and his T-shirts, just a certain smell which makes me think of Hugo. But before I had time to think much of that or anything, I fell asleep.

Chapter Sixteen

In the morning Daddy and I went out to buy me my present.

"Actually, I'm getting myself a present," Daddy said.

"What is it?" I said.

"A bicycle. The doctor says I need exercise, but tennis seems too exhausting and golf is obnoxious—so I thought maybe just bicycling."

"You could go in the park."

"Right. And I thought, if you like, I'll get you one too. Then we can go together."

"Great." I was really pleased. I had been thinking Daddy would just get me a pin or a blouse or something like that. I think he has good taste usually and gets things I like, but a bike would be even better.

We went to this big bike store on Broadway where you can rent bikes as well as buy them. Daddy had brought along a copy of *Consumer Reports* so he knew which one he wanted. He tried out the one for himself. It was funny seeing him on a bike. I just don't think of Daddy doing anything athletic. He doesn't seem the type.

"How does it feel, sir?" the man who was waiting on us asked when Daddy came to a stop.

"It feels magnificent," Daddy said, "and now I want the same model for this beautiful girl you see to my left."

"For a beautiful girl like that we have only the best," the man said.

"She's my daughter," Daddy said.

"You're a very lucky man," the man said.

"I certainly am," Daddy said.

I get so embarrassed when grownups talk like that, but I guess they always do.

"Okay, D.D., give it a try," Daddy said as the man wheeled out a beautiful blue ten-speed bicycle.

I felt a little nervous getting on it. It was so shiny and new—what if I fell over? But I didn't. I rode just down to the end of the block and back. "It's fine," I said.

"Will you take them with you?" the man said.

"We will," Daddy said. "Add it up and we'll ride them away!" He peeled off a lot of dollars and gave them to the man.

"Isn't that horribly expensive?" I whispered while we waited for the change.

"A mere pittance," Daddy said. Daddy is like that. I know he worries about money, but when he's with me and I even say I like a blouse I see in a store window, he'll say, "Let's go in and buy six of them in different colors." Mom says that's very unrealistic and it's just because Daddy was really poor when he was little and never got over it. I know that when I was little I thought Daddy was the richest man in the world because he always said, "Anything you want, you can have!" Now I know that isn't true, of course.

"But can we still afford things?" I asked as we were wheeling our bikes to the park. "I thought that since you were sick—"

"Honey, I'm not bedridden. I have to slow down

that's all. I'm not going on welfare. Anyway, in a couple of years I expect you to be out supporting me, and I'll just sit on the rocker on my back porch and smoke my corncob pipe."

I giggled. "You don't have a back porch, Daddy."

"I'll get one."

"You don't smoke a pipe."

"I'll start."

We rode all through the park. It was beautiful, not too hot, but warm enough so we didn't need jackets. The bike was wonderful—you hardly felt like you were riding it, it went so smoothly. I rode along beside Daddy and thought of being with Arlo the night before and I felt so good. I started thinking: right this minute, now, I feel happy. And then I thought of that Ingmar Bergman movie and the woman who dies and how she thought that.

When Daddy and I stopped to rest, I tried to tell him about that.

"But what's wrong with being conscious of how you feel?" Daddy said. His face was all pink from the bike riding because he has such fair skin.

"Well, maybe you're fooling yourself," I said. I couldn't exactly explain what I meant. "Maybe you should feel it, but not think about it."

Daddy was lying on the grass, his arms under his head. "I don't know," he said. "I think some people are born to reflect on what they do . . . and, well, maybe they lose something, some kind of spontaneity, but maybe they gain something too. . . . I wouldn't worry about it, love."

"I do," I said, pulling up some grass.

"You worry too much. You shouldn't. I feel you're too young for that." He sat up.

I chewed on some grass. "Daddy, if my marks go down this semester, though, is that okay? Because I feel I just—I couldn't concentrate, I kept—"

"I want them to go down!" Daddy said.

"Daddy, come on."

"No, I mean it. Nell, you're much too much of a worrier for a twelve-year-old."

"Thirteen!"

"For sixteen, even! I'm like that myself so I don't blame you."

"It's my Jewish genes," I said, smiling.

"Maybe, maybe, who knows? But why not try and take life as it comes. Fail a few subjects."

"I can't. I'll never be like *that*."

"Get a *C*, then—at least one *C*."

"I'll try," I said.

Actually, I think I may get a *C* in English because I know I didn't do well on the final at all.

We rode some more and then, around four o'clock, came back to the apartment for dinner. We just had roast chicken that Daddy had bought already cooked, but it was good.

Chapter Seventeen

I ended up getting a *B* in English. I did do badly on the exam, but Mrs. Pontoon took me aside and said that my work during the year had been so good she raised my grade. "I know this has been a hard year for you," she said.

Mrs. Pontoon has long brown hair that she wears loose, and glasses. I like her. "Now everything is okay," I said. Up till now I hadn't talked about the thing with Daddy to anyone at school except Heather. Maybe some of the teachers knew, but they didn't say anything.

I told her about Daddy having to exercise and how we both had bikes now.

"Maybe I'll see you in the park," she said. "I go out with Dudley every Saturday."

"Who is Dudley?"

"My son—he's fifteen months. He sits in a basket in back."

"Aren't you afraid he'll fall out?"

"No. Anyway, he's tough. He falls a million times a day and he just pulls himself back up again."

The last day of school I went home with Heather. Mom had said I could stay at her house that one night; Deirdre and Sharon are away. Heather is going to a special camp this summer which has a lot of dance and drama. She's very excited about it.

When we got to her house, her mother came out. "Hi, Nell!"

I felt embarrassed, seeing her. I wonder if she ever suspected about that night at the Sherry Netherland. But she seemed friendly. Heather says her mother doesn't know which end is up. I wonder.

Heather flung herself on one of the beds. "This is the best week of my whole life," she said. "The house is so quiet! It's great!"

"Are you getting ready for camp already?"

"Mentally. . . . But it doesn't start till June so I have a whole month."

"You could come out and stay with us, if you want."

"I'll ask Mom."

"Heath—"

"Um?"

"Did she really never suspect about that night?"

"With the baby-sitting?"

"Yes."

"Oh, maybe. She's all in a dither about Deirdre anyway. I don't think she had time to think much about it."

"What's with Deirdre?"

"Oh, she wants to marry this guy and he's around fifty-five—older than Dad, in point of fact—and he's been married twice. It's all kind of grisly, but every night there's a big family powwow about it."

"Do you think they'll let her?"

"Well, she's eighteen, so they can't very well stop her. Frankly, I think they suit each other perfectly. He's this really greasy guy with a huge car which he trades in every year, and he keeps boasting about how he used to earn four hundred thousand a year and he gave it all to his ex-wife and now he's cut down and is only earning a hundred thousand."

"Does she love him?"

"Probably. They'll sit there and count all their little possessions and be as happy as bugs. And she'll be out of the house which is the main thing."

"Lucky you."

"Lucky me, is right. Did Arlo come to the hotel that night?"

I nodded.

"Did you make out?"

I turned red. "Oh . . . vaguely."

"Vaguely! What does that mean?"

"Well, we kissed each other and that kind of thing."

Heather sat up. "What kind of thing?"

"No, just kissing, that was all."

"Was it nice?"

"Very."

Heather leaned back. "I love kissing," she said.

"Me too. I wish there wasn't all the rest of it, though."

"The rest isn't that bad." She smiled enigmatically.

"Heather!"

"Well, it isn't."

"What rest of it do you mean?"

"Oh, don't get excited. I'm still a virgin, for what that's worth, and probably will be for ages."

"Don't you wish you could just wake up and find you weren't, that you knew it all?"

"No," Heather said.

"How come?"

"Well, I think it's nice to find out slowly."

"But don't you feel scared?"

She shook her head. "Jack knows what's he's doing. He doesn't want to rush things."

I thought of that. I don't think Arlo knows much more than me. In a way I don't mind that.

"Did you ever talk with Deirdre and Sharon—like about what they did when they were our age and stuff like that?"

"Oh, Sharon would never talk about anything.

135

She's the type that locks the bathroom door just to get undressed. She's the type that worries about what her husband will think when he sees her in curlers for the first time."

"How about Deirdre?"

"Oh, she's just a nitwit. I think she's the type that thinks: first date—do this; second date—do that. Not if she likes him or anything. Just—tell me the rules and I'll follow them."

"How does she know what the rules *are?* Sometimes I wish there were still rules."

"Who knows? She reads Ann Landers or something."

"Heath—"

"What?"

"You know one thing I can never understand."

"What?"

"How come they always say the boy will lose respect for you if you sleep with him? Why shouldn't the girl lose respect for the boy?"

Heather laughed. "You're right . . . I never thought of that. Roger, I'm sorry, but I simply cannot see you again. I've lost all respect for you."

I laughed so much I got a side ache. I made Heather promise not to say anything funny for at least ten minutes.

Chapter Eighteen

Heather has to buy some things for camp. I agreed to go with her. I think her mother gave us kind of a funny glance when we borrowed her charge plates. Maybe she was thinking we would pull something funny again, like we did with the labels for the blouses.

"We'll be good, Mom," said Heather in a kind of pretend innocent way.

"Now Heather, I wasn't even going to mention that."

"We learned our lesson," Heather said, but there was a little smile on her face.

"Heather!"

"We did, Mom, really and truly. We'll never never—"

"I trust Nell to have more sense than you," Mrs. McCormmach said. "You keep an eye on her, Nell."

"Listen to that!" Heather said when we were out of the house. "She trusts *you* more than *me!*"

"Oh, parents are always like that," I said. "Daddy trusts you more than me. He always says how innocent you look."

137

Heather grinned. "I do, don't I? Jack says I look like I came fresh from the farm."

It was a beautiful day, very hot but not as muggy as New York sometimes is in May. We walked all the way down Fifth Avenue.

"Should we revisit the scene of our crime?" Heather said, meaning Saks where we had cut all the labels out.

"No! Can't we go somewhere else? I would feel they might have found out and remember us."

"Let's go to Lord and Taylor's, then."

At Lord and Taylor's Heather really just needed T-shirts. We went to the boys' department because she said they're cheaper there and fit her just as well. I don't think that many boys are built like Heather, but she just got a big size. I could see lots of boys were staring at her as she tried one on. Heather doesn't like dressing rooms. She just pulls things over her head and if they fit more or less all right, she takes them.

"Don't you need anything?" she said.

"Well, maybe a basket for the bike Daddy bought me. But I don't feel like getting it now."

"You're so lucky to have a bike. I'm going to try to get Deirdre to leave me her old one if she does marry old Grease Ball."

"Will she have a big wedding and all that, do you think?"

"Probably. You'd think it would be funny for him, his third marriage, going through the whole bit all over again."

"I guess men don't mind. Maybe you'll be a bridesmaid."

"Ugh."

"You could get a pretty dress."

"I hate those long itchy dresses," Heather said. "If I ever get married, I'm going to wear slacks and a shirt."

"Really?" I admire Heather so much for always knowing exactly what she will do years ahead.

138

Imagine even knowing what you would wear if you got married. Sometimes I think I would like an old-fashioned dress. I saw one in the window of this Mexican store on Lexington Avenue that had lace and long sleeves and it was really so pretty. Maybe Heather's right, though—it wouldn't be that practical.

Even though we didn't need to buy anything more, we browsed around in the teen department. "Isn't it weird to be teen-agers?" I said.

Heather shrugged.

"I feel like we should feel completely different, don't you?"

Heather pointed to the two girls in front of us trying on coats. One had purple lipstick and no eyebrows—she must have shaved them off. The other had hair cut so short she looked like she just came out of prison. "Is that what we should look like?" Heather said.

"No! Do you think we will?"

"Of course not."

In the teen-age department they had some really odd clothes, the kind you never imagine real people buying, but there were lots of girls roaming around looking at things. A lot of them had those very high clog shoes that always look so uncomfortable to me. It's funny how suddenly just because you're thirteen you're a special thing, a teen-ager, when up to then you haven't been anything special at all. I used to look forward to it, when I was eight or nine, and my baby-sitters were the age I am now. Now it seems like it doesn't matter that much.

We wandered down to the main floor and looked at some jewelry.

"I should get something for Mom," Heather said. "It's her birthday next week."

"Is it fair to get it on her charge?" I said. "I mean, that way she's paying for her own present."

"True, but in point of fact, Dad earns the money so it all comes from him anyway."

139

"My mother earns more than my father," I said, looking at a strange necklace which was of a wooden apple that looked as though someone had taken a bite out of it.

"Does he mind?"

"He says no. Anyway, she just puts it in the bank. She doesn't spend it on fancy things."

"Umm."

Heather was looking at some gold pins in a display case in front of us. I looked up and suddenly there, way at the end of the counter, I saw Arden. She had her big dark sunglasses on, but otherwise she looked the same. She was wearing a green dress. I guess she was buying something because she handed something to the saleslady and then just stood there, looking ahead of her. I prayed she wouldn't see me. But it's funny—the thing I thought of, seeing her there, was that time in the hotel room, not Daddy's throwing the phone at her, but right afterward when she suddenly took off her nightie, stood there stark naked and then got dressed and left. What was odd was seeing her without any clothes on. Somehow if you see someone you know well without their clothes, like, say, if I see Heather or Mom or Hugo, I don't give it a second thought. Their body just seems part of them, not especially different or anything. But it's strange to see the body of someone you don't know that well. It was as though Mrs. Pontoon had suddenly, before an English class, taken all her clothes off.

What was strange, too, was that I guess Arden could have been my stepmother, and yet now we wouldn't even say hello and maybe if I meet her in ten years we won't even remember each other. Yet there she was in her green dress and dark glasses. It gave me a funny feeling.

Heather looked up. "Hey, isn't that—"

I nudged her. "Ssh."

Outside the store I said, "I just didn't want her to see us."

"Why?"

"It would just be awkward."

"I thought you said your Dad wasn't seeing her anymore."

"That's why."

Heather seemed to understand that. At least she was quiet a few minutes and when she began to talk again, it was about something completely different.

Chapter Nineteen

In two weeks Hugo and I will go to the house on Long Island that Daddy has rented for July. August we will come back and stay with Mom and Greta, since August is when Mom gets her vacation. She gets three weeks.

Hugo really likes Greta now. Maybe it's because they are together all day long while Mom is at work. Maybe it's because she takes him fishing and makes him feel like he's a big help instead of a pest. One morning he said to me, "I'm going to marry Mommy and Greta when I grow up."

"You can't do that," I said.

"Why?" We were walking down to the lake where Greta had told us to meet her for lunch.

"Then you would be a bigamist," I said.

Hugo was quiet a minute. "Greta *is* big," he said finally.

"It's not a matter of size," I said.

"She's very *very* big," he said. "She's almost six feet tall!" He thought a minute more. "But when I grow up, I'm going to be bigger than that. I might be six feet two, like Daddy."

"You might," I said. I just cannot imagine Hugo

being six feet two, though I know it's perfectly possible.

"I'll be much bigger than *you*, he said.

"Who says?"

"Boys are always bigger than girls."

"They are not. Anyway, being a bigamist has nothing to do with being big, dope head. It means a man who has two wives."

"Oh."

It was real summer now. The grass was so thick we had to lift our legs high to walk over it. Down by the lake I could see Greta with her straw hat and her fishing rod and her lunch basket.

"It should be called a two-a-me," Hugo said.

"You may be right," I said. I rumpled his curls.

"Greta!" Hugo yelled. Suddenly he took off like a shot and went scrambling down to the lake shore.

Slowly, I followed him. There was plenty of time.

AVON ◆ CONTEMPORARY READING
FOR YOUNG PEOPLE

☐ **Pictures That Storm Inside My Head**
    Richard Peck, ed.   30080 $1.25

☐ **Don't Look and It Won't Hurt**
    Richard Peck   30668 $1.25

☐ **Dreamland Lake**   Richard Peck   30635 $1.25

☐ **Through a Brief Darkness**
    Richard Peck   21147 $ .95

☐ **Go Ask Alice**   33944 $1.50

☐ **A Hero Ain't Nothin' but a Sandwich**
    Alice Childress   33423 $1.50

☐ **It's Not What You Expect**   Norma Klein   32052 $1.25

☐ **Mom, the Wolfman and Me**
    Norma Klein   34405 $1.25

☐ **Johnny May**   Robbie Branscum   28951 $1.25

☐ **Blackbriar**   William Sleator   22426 $ .95

☐ **Run**   William Sleator   32060 $1.25

☐ **Soul Brothers and Sister Lou**
    Kristin Hunter   28175 $1.25

☐ **A Teacup Full of Roses**
    Sharon Bell Mathis   20735 $ .95

☐ **An American Girl**   Patricia Dizenzo   31302 $1.25

Where better paperbacks are sold or directly from the publisher.
Include 25¢ per copy for postage and handling; allow 4-6 weeks for delivery.

Avon Books, Mail Order Dept.
250 West 55th Street, New York, N.Y. 10019

CR 5-77